T0318320

Inspecting Psychology

Inspecting Psychology takes a sleuth's magnifying glass to the interplay between psychology, psychiatry and detective fiction to provide a unique examination of the history of psychology. As psychology evolved over the centuries, so did crime writing. This book looks at how the psychological movements of the time influenced classic authors from Agatha Christie and Arthur Conan Doyle to Dorothy Sayers and Georges Simenon, to reveal an enduring connection between psychology and the human need to solve mysteries.

Some key puzzles. Why did Agatha Christie make so many doctors killers in her books? Why did Simenon not become a psychiatrist? Did Lord Peter Wimsey have all the charm, passion and tenderness no lover gave Dorothy Sayers?

Beginning with the earliest origins of psychology in Greek literature alongside the Oedipal story and the ideas of Aristotle, the book travels through to the late 18th and 19th centuries and the work of Edgar Allan Poe who wrote the first detective story proper. With the birth of modern psychology in the late 19th century, the growing fascination with understanding behaviour coincided with the popular whodunnit. Readers are whisked through the development of psychology in the 20th century and beyond, from the impact of shell shock in the First World War and the early understanding of mental illness through to the growth of psychoanalysis and the ideas of Freud, behaviourism and attachment theory. At every stop on this original rattle through history, David Cohen reveals the influence these psychological movements had on crime writers and their characters and plots.

The result is a highly enjoyable, engaging read for those interested in how the unique pairing of the history of psychology with the history of the detective novel can unveil insights into the human condition. It should appeal to anyone interested in psychology who wants their subject served with a thriller on the side.

David Cohen got his Ph.D. on what makes children laugh. His latest books are *Churchill and Attlee: The Unlikely Allies Who Won the War* and *Surviving Lockdown: Human Nature in Social Isolation,* which was written in a hurry when we thought the pandemic would soon be over. If only. He is also a film-maker. His ITV film on the Soham murders was nominated for the Baftas. He produced *London Unplugged,* ten short films about London, and is planning to make a feature film based on his book *The Escape of Sigmund Freud,* the story of how Freud got out of Vienna in 1938.

Inspecting Psychology

How the Rise of Psychological Ideas Influenced the Development of Detective Fiction

David Cohen

Routledge
Taylor & Francis Group

LONDON AND NEW YORK

First published 2022
by Routledge
2 Park Square, Milton Park, Abingdon, Oxon OX14 4RN

and by Routledge
605 Third Avenue, New York, NY 10158

Routledge is an imprint of the Taylor & Francis Group, an informa business

© 2022 David Cohen

The right of David Cohen to be identified as author of this work has been asserted by him in accordance with sections 77 and 78 of the Copyright, Designs and Patents Act 1988.

British Library Cataloguing-in-Publication Data
A catalogue record for this book is available from the British Library

Library of Congress Cataloging-in-Publication Data
Names: Cohen, David, 1946- author.
Title: Inspecting psychology : how the rise of psychological ideas influenced the development of detective fiction / David Cohen.
Description: Abingdon, Oxon ; New York : Routledge, [2022] | Includes bibliographical references and index.
Identifiers: LCCN 2021019996 (print) | LCCN 2021019997 (ebook) | ISBN 9780367362218 (hardback) | ISBN 9780367362188 (paperback) | ISBN 9780429344664 (ebook)
Subjects: LCSH: English fiction--19th century--History and criticism. | Psychology and literature. | English fiction--20th century--History and criticism.
Classification: LCC PR878.P75 C64 2020 (print) | LCC PR878.P75 (ebook) | DDC 823.809355--dc23
LC record available at https://lccn.loc.gov/2021019996
LC ebook record available at https://lccn.loc.gov/2021019997

ISBN: 978-0-367-36221-8 (hbk)
ISBN: 978-0-367-36218-8 (pbk)
ISBN: 978-0-429-34466-4 (ebk)

DOI: 10.4324/9780429344664

Typeset in Sabon
by MPS Limited, Dehradun

Contents

Preface

In 1987 I waited for a car outside my flat in central London. It would stop just for a moment. An hour earlier the Court of Appeal had declared the convictions of the Guildford Four unsafe. Paul Hill, Gerry Conlon, Carole Richardson and Patrick Armstrong had been found guilty of bombing the Horse and Groom pub in Birmingham in 1974. Five people died. At their trial Mr Justice Donaldson regretted the defendants could not be tried for treason, the only offence to still carry the death penalty.

The car I was waiting for was bringing Patrick Armstrong to my flat which would be safe from the press and protesters. His family was sitting in the living room waiting for him.

I had been asked to offer a "safe house" by Dr James MacKeith, a psychiatrist who had worked at Brixton Prison and Broadmoor. He was an excellent clinician who also was skilful politically. His research with Gisli Gudjuddson, an Icelandic detective turned psychologist, had persuaded the Court of Appeal that the four had made false confessions under physical and psychological pressure. Their work was seen as a landmark in psychiatric research.

The landmark was not that new, however. Fifty years earlier Agatha Christie had made false confessions central to the plot of *The ABC Murders*. Alexander Cust admitted to killing Anne Archer in Andover, Betty Barnard in Bexhill, Sir Carmichael Clarke in Churston and a final victim in Doncaster. Headlines screamed "Cust is a maniac." The killings were senseless. Cust does not remember killing anyone but believes he must have done so. Poirot meets him and sees that Cust is no man to plan or execute such "clever" murders. He is neurotic, very suggestible and pathetic. A smart and ruthless murderer has manipulated events so that Cust is always present where the murders took place near the time they took place. He had been a victim of shell

shock in the 1914 war and is subject to fits. In the end, Poirot solves
the mystery and absolves Cust. Fiction had anticipated psychology and
psychiatry by half a century.

I do not know if either James MacKeith or Gisli Gudjuddson
read detective novels much, but MacKeith told me he became
interested in how people came to make false confessions after
working in Brixton Prison and then in Broadmoor.

Psychologists have studied many esoteric aspects of life. One of my
favourites is how human beings and octopi remember underwater.
Researchers have also devoted careers to studying gambling, the way
instruments can mislead pilots, the motivation of athletes and much
else. Liam Hudson, author of the classic *Contrary Imaginations*, which
studied the creativity of schoolchildren, once complained psychology
concentrated too much on abnormal rather than normal behaviour.
Reading detective novels is normal given that millions of copies sell
each year yet there has been no work on the way psychology and
psychiatry have influenced detective stories, even though these often
raise disturbing psychological questions. There is an obvious parallel
between the detective and the psychoanalyst; both seek hidden truths.
The guilty obviously don't want to be found out, and the unconscious
is shy about its secrets.

For a writer the first challenge is to make readers read on. So
here is my attention grabber.

"Reader, I murdered him."

The phrase is homage to Charlotte Bronte's classic *Jane Eyre*. Its
most famous line is "Reader I married him." As we shall see *Jane
Eyre* has a long legacy. I see no reason to let readers escape a probe
into motives. So,

Have you thought of killing someone? Never? Be honest.

In what circumstances?

Have you planned, even daydreamed, how you might do it?

Do these thoughts slink out in dreams, slip-ups and the mistakes
that Freud described in *The Psychopathology of Everyday Life?*

More than half of those questioned in a survey in New Zealand in
2016 admitted they had thought of killing someone – and those
most likely to do it scored high on narcissism, psychopathy and poor
self-esteem. Men were twice more likely to think of killing than
women were. We all seem to carry a dagger in our soul, but there is
every difference, as Poirot often remarks, between wanting someone
dead and killing them. Today the Internet dangles temptation. A site
called Etsy advertises poison accessories such as strychnine, a poison

often used by Agatha Christie's killers. You can't buy strychnine in the U.K., but arsenic is legally available in various forms.

Reynolds and McCrea (2017) have studied the rather sparse work on when people think of killing. Inevitably their research on homicidal fantasies was carried out in a lab where there were no guns, poisons or knives to tempt them into action. In this "safe" environment, 63% of American undergraduates had "homicidal ideation." Their work is properly academic and so does not include the Inner Killer test I am devising where you find out how much you want to do away with your partner, brother, sister, boss. There are many tests of psychopathy which have been reasonably well validated.

This book also raises less personal questions:

Are detective novels so popular because they banish doubt?

Does it feel satisfying when they pin the guilt on someone definite?

How many people commit murder and never get found out?

Scotland Yard detectives have hundreds of unsolved murders on their books. Jack the Ripper is the most famous, while 40% of homicides in America are never solved.

In terms of murderous fantasies, George Axelrod's wonderful black comedy *How to Murder Your Wife* is a masterpiece. It was made in the 1950s, a very different era when attitudes to domestic violence were complacent.

Jack Lemmon plays a cartoonist who prides himself on acting out everything in his comic strip. His valet, played by Terry Thomas, hates the fact that his master's new stunning Italian wife has disturbed their cosy masculine domestic routine; the valet encourages him to draw a strip where he dumps the wife in the "glopiter glopiter" machine, so named because it is the sound the cement mixer makes. When that strip is published, the wife has disappeared. Lemmon had the arrogance to advertise the murder he committed in a nationally syndicated cartoon strip. The police arrest him, and he is tried for murder.

In court, Lemmon sacks his hen-pecked lawyer and asks the jury – made up of married men – to imagine a button in front of them. He draws it. We see it in close up.

Press the button. Without causing your wife any pain, she disappears. Poof! Vanished. She can never nag you again about staying out late, or flirting with your secretary, or moaning about how much she spends on clothes.

Press the button. No need to do anything more, let alone anything violent. The jury peers at the tempting button. So how many of the 12 men and true will press it?

They all do. Even the judge.

1950s' Hollywood could not bear too much reality. So in the end, Lemmon is reunited with his wife who ran off after she had seen a draft of the cartoon strip. Feeling betrayed – no wonder – she went home to Italy, but her mother persuaded to go back to her husband. Lemmon is delighted to see her. The comedy shines some lights on some of the dark places of our minds – especially the violence that lurks in the male mind.

You don't always know where the idea for a book comes from.

When I came to England in 1956 as a ten-year-old, I needed to understand this strange country my parents had fled to. (We were not persecuted Jews. My uncle had forged gold coins which the Swiss authorities did not appreciate, so our family had to get out fast.)

I went to a prep school near Sloane Square. Some of the teachers were quite openly violent. The maths teacher, a colonel in the 1945 war who still called himself colonel, flung lighted matches at us in the hope of setting someone's hair on fire. I learned years later that his wife had bed hopped from one end of Sloane Square to the other. The English are sometimes stereotyped as being cold, but the passions in Christie's books are often intense. She was very alive to the power of sexuality.

Another teacher relished beating us with a Jokari bat for any excuse at all. I eventually became head boy. As such when one of our teachers disappeared after a cricket match I had to lead boys back to Sloane Square. The next day the whole school was caned, except me. I had shown leadership. Why there was such mass punishment was never explained.

By the time I was 12 I had started to read Agatha Christie's books partly because they seemed so English. By the late 1950s, the society they described had been changed by the war, but I did not realise that. The typical Christie book is set in a country house or a village. No one is really hard up. The vicar bores his congregation. The leading characters have servants, and even Miss Marple, whose nephew often treats her to holidays, has a maid. One exception to this picture-postcard Englishness is *A Caribbean Holiday* where some important characters are black. Miss Marple solves that crime deftly.

Many immigrants, as I was, try hard not just to understand the English but to be accepted as one of them. I was lucky in coming to London when I was young enough to speak the language without a foreign accent. Understanding the subtleties of the English class system, a theme in many detective novels, was harder.

This book does summarise some plots. The only time I worked out who the killer was in a Christie was in *Death in the Clouds*. The answer comes later in the book. Somehow in 2018 an idea appeared in my mind. In what ways had Christie and other classic detective writers, like Dorothy Sayers, been influenced not just by Freud, but by psychology and psychiatry in general? Gladys Mitchell even made her sleuth Mrs Bradley a psychoanalyst – and the books have become a stylish TV series. Frank Tallis is a clinical psychologist who has set a number of mysteries in Vienna in Freud's day. His detective Max Liebermann is also a psychiatrist. Priests do well as fictional detectives as they are trained to hear confessions. I have searched but so far one of the few professions which does not boast a fictional detective is chiropody. Odd since footprints are often a clue.

I had intended to limit this book to English-language writers, but I read some of Simenon's Maigret books. No other detective writer was as interested in and influenced by psychiatric ideas. He even set one book in the Bicetre, one of Paris' ancient asylums. The book includes some summaries of novels. I have tried to limit these summaries by featuring the influence of psychology in them.

Some commentators claim there are only a few motives for murder – greed, sex, fear, revenge, jealousy and religious hatred – one less than the *Seven Deadly Sins* as the slothful cannot summon up the energy to kill anybody. As we shall see, some writers were more ingenious. Gladys Mitchell's Mrs Bradley killed once at least for altruistic reasons. Agatha Christie also allowed Poirot to commit a moral murder in his last case *Curtains*. But these are exceptions to the usual three Ls – lust, lucre and loathing – as motives.

Psychologists have identified various drives and needs which echo these motives. All humans are driven to find safety; most also want to procreate and to succeed. Maslow's hierarchy of needs starts with the basic – food, water, safety – and moves up to self-esteem which often involves making money, and finally caps with it with "self-actualisation," or finding your true identity. The French philosopher Jean-Paul Sartre makes two of his characters find their true identity when they kill.

This book does not pretend to be a comprehensive history of psychology, but it looks at those psychologists whose ideas are most relevant to detective writing. It starts with Aristotle, who first stressed the importance of the association of ideas, a theory developed by David Hume. Since sleuths often find the killer through spotting unlikely associations, it is surprising no one has turned Aristotle into a detective, especially as there have been many thrillers set in ancient Greece. Finding the guilty completes a pattern which makes a strong link between Gestalt psychology and the whodunnit. The brain likes puzzles.

The occult often featured in detective stories in the 1920s and 1930s, so Chapter 4 looks at the work of William James who was president of the Society for Psychical Research in the 1890s. Clark Hull who studied hypnosis was also a pioneer of learning theory. Hypnosis often occurs in the detective story.

In the 1930s, three men dominated French psychology and psychiatry – the often irritatingly obscure Jacques Lacan, Jean-Paul Sartre and the child psychologist Jean Piaget. Sartre said, "Hell is other people" which could serve as a motto for many murderers. Perhaps, though, one less well-known psychoanalyst, John Bowlby, had even more impact. His theory of attachment emphasised the bond between mother and child. Deny the child that bond and he or she is maimed. And the maimed seek revenge. A number of Christie's books involve adults who were abandoned or hurt as children and return to seek revenge.

The Silence of the Lambs and *Mindhunter* could not exist if were not for the FBI. In 1972 it formed the Behavioural Science Unit which compiled a centralised database on serial offenders. Agents travelled to prisons across the United States to interview serial killers and obtain information about:

- Motives
- Planning and preparation
- Details of the crimes
- Disposal of evidence (e.g. bodies and murder weapons)

Three of these depend on observing and reporting behaviour.

The FBI unit is psychologically sophisticated and has inspired many books, fiction and nonfiction.

This book examines a variety of themes – the history of psychology, literary history, the history of psychiatry and psychoanalysis, the history of the detective novel, the relationship of writers to their characters and the chutzpah of a few psychoanalysts who claim authors gave the wrong solution to some of their works.

Spoiler Alert

I have put in italics the detailed description which some readers may prefer to skip because they want to read the book in full without knowing the solution.

The author does not know best – or anything at all.

Among the psychoanalysts who have rewritten whodunnits, Professor Pierre Bayard of the University of Paris gets top prize. He has revised Conan Doyle's *The Hound of the Baskervilles* and Christie's *The Murder of Roger Ackroyd* and *And Then There Were None*. Bayard is an expert on interpretation – a quick bow to Freud's *The Interpretation of Dreams* perhaps – and his re-interpretations claim that the original authors were duped by their own unconscious. If they had been psychoanalysed they would never have made the mistakes they made. The philosopher A.J. Ayer made fun of Jean-Paul Sartre, who in his *Being and Nothingness* wrote "le neant s'aneanti" – which is often translated as "the nothing nothings itself," which seems to mean, well, nothing. Ayer huffed the sentence was meaningless and sniped French philosophers were all too fond not just of the obscure, but of the utterly incomprehensible.

In his *How to Talk About Books You Haven't Read* Bayard argues there is no clear boundary between reading and non-reading and invites readers to build a freer relationship with the text. Bayard has a serious reputation in France and is also the author of the baffling *Anticipatory Plagiarism*. Call me an unimaginative empiricist but I can't work out how Shakespeare might be said to have plagiarised Ibsen as The Bard wrote 250 years earlier than the author of *Peer Gynt*. Bayard is impervious to such time travel quibbles and says, "What interests me in the literature is its undecidability. She and psychoanalysis are allied in the complex spaces they open up against a certain type of political discourse, today taken to caricature." Bayard argues the text is a space where writers and reader can communicate (or not).

Bayard has the brio to suggest Agatha Christie and Conan Doyle decided on the wrong killer in three of their books, and this is possible as the writer is not wholly the writer, or perhaps not really the writer at all.

This is not an academic book, however, and should not be forbidding, as those discussed are among the most readable authors of the last 200 years, including Agatha Christie, Arthur Conan Doyle, Georges Simenon, Dorothy Sayers and John Le Carre whose *A Murder of Quality* has the essential features of a whodunnit. George Smiley faces red herrings, an obvious suspect who could not have done it and finally discovers a surprising solution.

To speak of the author – the book – the reader is now seen *as a little simple as a* connection by literary critics. The flow according to literary theory is different.

The author – her or his books – readers' reactions to the books – revisions and new versions of the books by some readers who feel they can do better than the original writer.

What was once academic has become part of popular culture. Fans of *The Simpsons* know it glories in multiple intertextual references to literature, films, other TV shows. Intertextual simply means it refers to other texts. Psychoanalysis has seen similar developments, especially interpretations, reinterpretations and de-interpretations of classic texts as Jacques Lacan did with Freud.

As I refer to *Jane Eyre* a number of times it is worth noting the novel inspired The *Wide Sargasso Sea* by Jean Rhys which is intertextual as it develops a character in a previous text; Bertha Mason first appeared as the mad wife of Rochester who is locked in an attic.

The author addresses the reader as Jane Eyre did when she announced, "Reader I married him," after she and Rochester have made up. It was a sign of ancient simplicities that a book was something the author wrote and the reader read.

The structure of this book, however, is largely chronological. It traces the broad outlines of the history of psychology and in parallel the rise and rise of the whodunnit.

Chapter 1

The first psychologies

From rock art to the association of ideas

Julian Symons provided a history of the detective novel in *Bloody Murder,* but he hardly mentions what seems very peculiar. Why did no whodunnit appear before 1841? That was 2,400 years after the Greek tragedies that wallowed in violence and death, and Aristotle wrote the first textbook of psychology.

Like Greek tragedy, the Elizabethan theatre also filled the stage with bodies. Neither genre though ever left the audience in any doubt as to who was guilty. The "no mystery to it" killing starts with the first murder story in the fourth chapter of Genesis. When Cain kills Abel, the Bible says who and why. The *Old Testament* records many violent deaths, but there is no instance where we do not know who is guilty. Quite often it is Jehovah wiping out those who displeased the All-Mighty who has the insight to admit he is a jealous God. Jealous Jehovah was responsible for the drowning of the Egyptians in the Red Sea, not to mention the slaughter of Philistines, Hittites and many other tribes in the land of milk, honey and, in fact, blood.

Medieval literature also did not tantalise with puzzles. Dante's *The Divine Comedy* is a prime example. In the *Inferno,* murderers boil forever in a river of blood, but not all of them boil equally, so a thermometer might be handy. The degree of violence they used to kill determines the temperature of the blood they boil in. Some sinners are more boiled than others, in fact. The poem laments "blind cupidity and insane anger." Dante too, however, does not leave his readers with any question as to the identity of the many killers.

In Chaucer's *The Canterbury Tales,* no pilgrim mentions a body in the library or in the cathedral on the way to pray at the shrine of

DOI: 10.4324/9780429344664-1

Thomas a Becket. Becket was murdered, but there was no mystery as to the identity of the four knights who killed the archbishop. In *Murder in the Cathedral*, T.S. Eliot gave each of them speeches where they justified themselves. They had to do their duty, and their stiff upper lips stopped them moaning like a foreigner. So they accepted exile; they would miss England, but it was a consolation they had helped the Crown. Like Freud, T.S. Eliot liked detective books but did not try to write one.

Shakespeare's plays also drip with blood, but he too did not leave his audiences in any doubt as to the guilty. Richard III boasts, "Why I can smile and murder whilst I smile," and proceeds to do just that, ordering the deaths of the Princes in the Tower who threaten his claim to the throne. The killers are then killed themselves to make sure they never blab.

In *Hamlet*, that U R text of psychoanalysis, the Prince of Denmark changes after he has seen the ghost of his father who accuses his brother Claudius of poisoning him. Hamlet then turns detective. After some hesitation, and with the useful arrival of some ramshackle players who might have been called Wedoanyplay.com, Hamlet decides to test Claudius' guilt. He gets the players to stage *The Murder of Gonzago*, a play within the play, to see how his uncle responds when the king drips poison in his brother's ear. The device works.

When Gonzago dies, Claudius is no Richard III; he panics and stops the play. Hamlet finally accepts that his uncle killed his father and takes revenge after much hesitation. In *Macbeth* again there are no doubts. Lady Macbeth masterminds the murders her husband commits.

By 1616, when Shakespeare died of utterly natural causes, contemporary dramas staged killings by the blood bucket, but there was never any doubt as to who did it.

The fact that there was no whodunnit until 1840 is especially curious given the fact that the human brain loves puzzles. The brain is bombarded by sensations every nanosecond and "wants" to make sense of them. Sadly we have no idea of the prehistory of our interest in puzzles. The earliest examples of culture do not give much of a clue.

Ancestral artists

Around 44000 B.C., on the Indonesian island of Sulawesi, an artist sketched tiny, animal-headed hunters armed with spears cornering wild hogs and small buffaloes. These figures show that our ancestors already had imaginations much like our own. "We think of the ability for humans to make a story, a narrative scene, as one of the last steps of human cognition," according to Maxime Aubert, an archaeologist at Griffith University in Australia. "This is the oldest rock art in the world and all of the key aspects of modern cognition are there."

But Aubert is wrong about one aspect of human cognition; none of these paintings reveal why human beings love puzzles, let alone when that love began. The question first occurs in ancient Greek philosophy.

The first psychologies

The Greek historian Herodotus wrote that, in the 7th century B.C., the Egyptian pharaoh Psamtik I sent two infants to live with a shepherd in one of the most isolated parts of his kingdom, on the condition that they never be spoken to. According to Herodotus, the children repeatedly babbled the word *bekòs*, an ancient Phrygian word meaning "bread," leading Psamtik to believe that Phrygia rather than Egypt was mankind's oldest civilisation.

Aristotle made the first attempt at human psychology in his *Para Psyche*, "About the Mind." The mind was for him the "first entelechy," or primary reason for the existence and functioning of the body. His studies of zoology – he was the David Attenborough of his time – influenced his psychology. He argued there were three types of souls: the plant soul, the animal soul and the human soul, which gave human beings the unique ability to reason and create. Curiously he thought one did not need a body to think – the soul was sufficient.

Aristotle has to be considered in some detail. In *De Anima*, he studied whether all psychological states were also material states of the body. "This, it is necessary to grasp, but not easy" (*De Anima* i 1, 402a5). He then tried to provide an account of the activities of plants and animals, alongside those of humans. He insisted that because various psychological states, including anger, joy, courage, pity, loving and hating, all involve the body, the study of soul "is already in the province of the natural scientist" (*De Anima* i 1, 403a16–28). At the same time, however, the mind may not be enmeshed in the body in the same way as these sorts of states. So he denied that natural scientists could examine the study of soul in its entirety. This is presumably why in the opening chapter of *De Anima* Aristotle admitted he was unsure about the best method for investigating psychological matters (*De Anima* i 1, 402a16–22). If different sciences employ different methods and the study of soul is bifurcated so that it belongs to no one science, it will indeed be difficult to know how best to proceed in any inquiry concerning it. Aristotle was modest as well as brilliant and added: "Grasping anything trustworthy concerning the soul is completely and in every way among the most difficult of affairs" (*De Anima* i 1, 402a10–11).

In terms of the history of psychology, one of Aristotle's great contributions was that he saw the importance of the association of ideas. He wrote:

> When, therefore, we accomplish an act of Reminiscence, we pass through a certain series of precursive movements, until we arrive at a movement, on which the one we are in quest of is habitually consequent. Hence too it is, that we hunt through the mental train, excogitating from the present or some other, and from its similar or contrary or coadjacent. Through this process Reminiscence is effected. For the movements are, in these cases, sometimes at the same, sometimes at the same time, sometimes parts of the same whole; so that the subsequent movement is already more than half accomplished.
>
> —*Aristotle as translated by W. Hamilton*

To understand how we thought, we had to examine contiguity, similarity and contrast.

The most intuitive "detective" ever was the blind seer of Greek mythology Tiresias. Thebes, his city, is suffering from the plague. Oedipus the King asks Tiresias to help investigate who killed the previous king Laius. No one has been punished which may be provoking the anger of the gods. At first, Tiresias refuses and hints that Oedipus really does not want to find the killer. Oedipus replies that Tiresias' reputation is exaggerated and suggests the seer himself had some hand in the murder. The spitting mad seer then reveals that it was Oedipus himself who killed Laius.

Oedipus could be considered one of the first case histories in psychology. As a child, he was abandoned by his parents and left to die because they had heard the prophecy that he would kill his father and marry his mother. Fate interfered with the fates though, and a kind shepherd found him and brought him up.

As a young man, Oedipus felt he had to go to Thebes to find out who he really was but on the way, "where three roads meet," he killed an old man. A therapist might suggest he was acting out his anger at the father who abandoned him. Oedipus then goes to the city and marries Laius's widow Jocasta.

Sophocles' great play *Oedipus Rex* is not just a story of murder, as Laius was Oedipus' father, but also of incest as Jocasta is, in fact, his mother. Few commentaries, however, mention that Oedipus and Jocasta had a happy marriage until the plague hit the city. When he knows the truth Oedipus blinds himself. In some versions of the story, Jocasta hangs herself; in others, she commits suicide after one of her other sons dies.

Tiresias does not deduce like Holmes, Miss Marple, Poirot or Lord Peter Wimsey do. He does not need clues to winkle out the psychology of the individual. The not-so-kindly gods provide him with dreams and visions that reveal the truth. He does not need to find out – he knows.

The story has some elements of the whodunnit since we do not know at first who Oedipus is. Freud famously based his theory of the Oedipus complex on the myth whose uncomfortable truth was that, subconsciously, sons want to kill their fathers and sleep with their mothers.

The texts of Aristotle's works were lost during the Dark Ages and only rediscovered towards the end of the 13th century. Then there was a flurry of psychological writings. Avicenna, Thomas Aquinas, Albertus Magnus and Roger Bacon developed complex theories of mind. What we would now call cognition was understood as a two-part process, with physiological mechanisms in the brain mirrored by processes in the soul or mind. The brain transformed the "vital spirit" into the "animal spirit," which controlled sensation, movement, imagination, cognition and memory. No one knew how, and it is arguable we still do not. The mind-brain-body problem awaits a solution. Philosophers always studied their own mental processes.

An exception was James IV of Scotland, who was one of the few to conduct what we would now call an experiment. His love of languages led him to conceive of the kind of study only a king could. In 1493, he ordered two newborn babies to be sent to live on the isolated island of Inchkeith to be raised by a deaf-mute woman. They would not hear any language. His aim was to see what language the children acquired because as they heard no words, he believed that this language, whatever it might be, must surely be the innate, God-given language of mankind. The children somewhat improbably spoke their first words in Hebrew.

The 17th-century philosopher Thomas Hobbes accepted Aristotle's stress on association. He emphasised what he called, variously, the succession, sequence, series, consequence, coherence, train of imaginations or thoughts. But neither Aristotle, Aquinas nor Hobbes used the phrase that we are familiar with now. It was John Locke who introduced the phrase "association of ideas" as the title of a chapter in the fourth edition of his *Essay*.

In the empiricist tradition, Locke was followed by Bishop Berkeley who is famous for his maxim "*esse est percipi*," to be is to be perceived. It suggests a universe where things and people flip in and out of existence which would make for confusion. Luckily though, Berkeley concluded as he perhaps had to being a bishop, that God saw all the time as the Almighty never needed to sleep or even nap. Berkeley wrote:

> That one idea may suggest another to the mind, it will suffice that they have been observed to go together, without any demonstration of the necessity of their coexistence, or so much as knowing what it is that makes them so to coexist.
> *An Essay Towards a New Theory of Vision, § 25*

The next philosopher-psychologist of note was David Hume. He suggested that Berkeley should have been more explicit in his reference to association. Association is central to the success of detectives, of course. Poirot's little grey cells eventually hit on associations everyone else has missed. There is even a psychological test, the Remote Associations Test, nicely abbreviated to RAT, which reveals how well subjects make unlikely associations.

Hume spoke of association as a "kind of attraction which in the mental world will be found to have as extraordinary effects as in the natural, and to show itself in as many and as various forms" (*A Treatise of Human Nature*, i. 1, § 4).

Eleven years after Hume's *A Treatise of Human Nature*, David Hartley, another Scot, who was a physician, tried to combine his theory of association with a hypothesis as to the corresponding action of the nervous system. He based his idea on the suggestion of a vibratory motion within the nerves thrown out by Newton in the last paragraph of the *Principia*. Newton argued that an

electrical aether permeates the nerve and transmits vibrations along it. This implies that the nerve is a communication line, and potentially an extension of the mind.
Hartley said:

> Any sensations A, B, C, etc., by being associated with one another a sufficient number of times, get such a power over the corresponding ideas a, b, c, etc., that any one of the sensations A, when impressed alone, shall be able to excite in the mind b, c, etc., the ideas of the rest.

Hume suggested there was a regular order to our thoughts. If ideas occurred to us randomly, so that all our thoughts were "loose and unconnected," we wouldn't be able to think coherently (T 1.1.4.1/ 10). Coherence implied that was "a secret tie or union among particular ideas, which causes the mind to conjoin them more frequently, and makes the one, upon its appearance, introduce the other" (Abstract 35). Association was that tie. It was not "an inseparable connexion," but rather "a gentle force, which commonly prevails," by means of which one idea naturally introduces another (T 1.1.4.1/10).

In the first *Enquiry*, Hume stated that even though it is obvious to everyone that our ideas are connected in this way, he was the first philosopher who "attempted to enumerate or class all the principles of association" (EHU 3.2/24). He illustrated Maslow's need for self-esteem. Hume thought these "universal principles" as so distinctive that he advertised them as his most original contribution – one that entitles him call himself an *"inventor"* (Abstract 35).

Hume identified three principles of association: resemblance, contiguity in time and place, and causation. When someone shows you a picture of your best friend, you think of her because the picture *resembles* her. When you are reminded of something that happened in the 1960s – miniskirts, for example – you may think of the Vietnam War, because they are *temporally contiguous*. Thinking of the Tower of London may lead you to think of Tower Bridge since they are *spatially contiguous*. And then of Anne Boleyn who was beheaded there. *Causality* works both from cause to effect and effect to cause: meeting someone's father may make you think of his son; encountering the son may lead you to think of his father.

Causation is the strongest of these principles, and the only one that takes us "beyond our senses" (T 1.3.2.3/74). It established links between our present and past experiences and our expectations about the future, so that "all reasonings concerning matters of fact seem to be founded on the relation of *Cause* and *Effect*" (EHU 4.1.4/26). Taking aspirin in the past has relieved my headaches, so I expect that aspirin will soon relieve my present headache. Hume admitted that causation is the least understood of the associative principles, but promises, "we shall have occasion afterwards to examine it to the bottom" (T 1.1.4.2/11).

The associative principles are *original*, and their "effects are everywhere conspicuous," but their causes "are mostly unknown, and must be resolv'd into *original* qualities of human nature, which I pretend not to explain," Hume adds. Accordingly, we should curb any "intemperate desire" to account further for them, for doing so would take us illegitimately beyond the bounds of experience (T 1.1.4.6/12–13).

Hume doesn't try to explain *why* we associate ideas. He is interested only in establishing that we *do* associate ideas in these ways. Given that his claim that the associative principles explain the important operations of the mind is an empirical one, he admits that he cannot prove conclusively that his list of associative principles is complete. He may have missed something.

Hume concluded that it should be "easy to conceive of what vast consequences these principles must be in the science of human nature." Since they "are the only ties of our thoughts, they are really *to us* the cement of the universe, and all the operations of the mind must, in great measure, depend on them" (Abstract 35).

This book does chart some unlikely links. Hume spent years in Paris as secretary to the British embassy at a time when Voltaire was writing. And it was Voltaire who offered the first example of the kind of detection that would make Holmes, Poirot and others so popular.

The first detection

Voltaire's *Zadig* written in 1747 is not a detective novel but offers the first example of rational detection later sleuths marvelled audiences with. Zadig has retired to a country house by the Euphrates where he studies "the Nature and Properties of Animals and Plants." One day he meets one of the queen's eunuchs "seeking, with Impatience, for something lost of the utmost Importance."

The chief eunuch asks if Zadig has seen Her Majesty's dog. Zadig points out she is actually a bitch and adds: "And very small. ... She has had Puppies too lately; she's a little lame with her left Fore-foot and has long Ears." "By your exact Description, Sir, you must doubtless have seen her," says the eunuch. Zadig denies that; it is all a matter of deduction.

Zadig then is told that the king's best palfrey has broken loose and is asked if he has seen him. "No Horse," said Zadig,

> ever gallop'd smoother; he is about five Foot high, his Hoofs are very small; his Tail is about three Foot six Inches long; the studs of his Bit are of pure Gold, about 23 Carats; and his Shoes are of Silver, about Eleven penny Weight a-piece.

The eunuch assumes that Zadig has seen the animal and asks where the palfrey is. "I never sat Eyes on him," Zadig replies, and "neither did I ever hear before now, that his Majesty had such a Palfrey."

Zadig can only give such accurate descriptions, the eunuch believes, because he has stolen both animals. He is brought before the grand Desterham (the name is Babylonian) who sends him to "be confin'd for Life in some remote and lonely Part of Siberia." Voltaire was not sound on geography. It would take months to travel from the Euphrates to Siberia, but Zadig is soon whisked back from the north when the bitch and the palfrey are found. He then glories in explaining that he saw

> upon the Sand the Footsteps of an Animal, and I easily inferr'd that it must be a little one. The several small, tho' long Ridges of Land between the Footsteps of the Creature, gave me just Grounds to imagine it was a Bitch whose Teats hung down; and for that Reason, I concluded she had but lately pupp'd. As I observ'd likewise some other Traces, in some Degree different, which seem'd to have graz'd all the Way upon the Surface of the Sand, on the Side of the fore-Feet, I knew well enough she must have had long Ears.

Zadig also saw "prints made upon the Sand by a Horse's Shoes; and found that their Distances were in exact Proportion; from that Observation, I concluded the Palfrey gallop'd well." He also deduced the palfrey's tail was "three Foot and a half long, with which he had whisk'd off the Dust on both Sides as he ran along." Then under the trees, Zadig saw "leaves that had been lately fallen on the Ground," which allowed him to work out the height of the horse. Give the solution and explain how you got there – and you leave the audience agog as Zadig does. "The whole Bench of Judges stood astonish'd at the Profundity of Zadig's nice Discernment."

In *The Name of the Rose*, Umberto Eco pilfered this episode when his hero, William of Baskerville, approaches the monastery that is the scene of the first of many killings. Baskerville, his name a nod to Conan Doyle's famous *The Hound of the Baskervilles*, meets the abbey's cellarer who is looking for a horse.

Baskerville tells the astonished cellarer it must be the abbot's horse; there would not be such a posse of monks trying to find it otherwise. He then describes Brunellus perfectly as black, 5 feet tall and with a sumptuous tail. Adso, the young monk who is with Baskerville, marvels at the older man's skill. Baskerville explains he had seen some broken twigs; their height on the trees told him the height of the horse.

Finally, the horse would be called Brunellus as that was then the most popular name for a horse. Eco did not acknowledge his debt to Voltaire or that Baskerville was a superb example of the priest as sleuth.

The birth of criminal investigation

It has been suggested that one reason there were no detective novels before the late 19th century was that there were no detectives. In fact, there had been officials whose job was to catch criminals for centuries long before. The Statute of Winchester of 1285, for example, decreed local communities had to raise a hue and cry to find wrongdoers, and that "the whole hundred shall be answerable for any theft or robbery." By the 14th century, the office of constable was well established. Shakespeare made fun of them as plodders, writing characters such as Dogberry, Dull and Elbow; all are self-important and incompetent.

By the 1730s, towns often paid constables to patrol at night. In 1737, an Act of Parliament was passed "for better regulating the Night Watch of the City of London" and specified the number of paid constables who should be on duty each night. The author of *Tom Jones*, Henry Fielding, established the Bow Street Runners in 1749. *Tom Jones* is a brilliant novel, but hardly a whodunnit.

One possible answer to the puzzle of why the whodunnit arrived so late is that death was ever-present in the Middle Ages, most dramatically when the Black Death raged. Also, death was perhaps less final because it was not the end of one's being. You might be upped to heaven or downed to hell for all eternity. The French historian Philippe Aries has argued that before the 17th century, men and women were acutely aware of their own imminent death and prepared for it. For example, Tristan and Lancelot followed established rituals. Lancelot positioned his body with his face towards Jerusalem and waited. As they were dying, many Christians lay on their backs, facing the heavens. Death was a public ceremony; parents, spouses, family, neighbours and even children were present. In the 11th and 12th centuries, Aries argues, the individual rather than the act of death became the centre of attention. At the same time, there were more depictions of corpses and skeletons.

When seeing the dead was so normal and, less final as everyone believed in an afterlife, the crucial unknown was; was one going to heaven, hell or purgatory? Not who had caused the death.

From the mid-18th century, Gothic novels and melodramas were popular but again, there was no mystery as to the identity of the killer. Audiences were not led on a clue splattered journey to find the guilty. It would not be until the middle of the 19th century that a writer asked readers to solve the puzzle of who had done it.

Chapter 2

Psychology, phrenology and psychiatry

The late 18th–19th centuries and the work of Edgar Allen Poe

In the 1970s, Mao Tse Tung's second in command Chou en Lai was asked what was the legacy of the French Revolution of 1789; "it is too early to tell," he said. His remark was designed to intrigue, but it was not so odd because the events of 1789 were so extraordinary. The revolution led to bloodletting, cruelty and the innovation of the guillotine because so many executioners were inefficient; it also led to advances in psychiatry.

In 1792, Pinel became the chief physician at the Bicetre Hospital in Paris, the setting 150 years later for one of the Maigret stories. In 1797, Pussin first freed patients of their chains and banned physical punishment, although straitjackets could be used instead.

Patients were allowed to move freely about the hospital grounds, and eventually dark dungeons were replaced with sunny, well-ventilated rooms. Pussin's and Pinel's approaches were remarkably successful, and they later brought similar reforms to a mental hospital in Paris, la Salpetriere. Pinel's successor, Jean Esquirol (1772–1840), went on to help establish ten new asylums that operated on the same principles. There was an emphasis on the selection and supervision of attendants who would establish a suitable setting to facilitate psychological work. This revolutionary move anticipated the anti-psychiatrist R.D. Laing by two centuries; when ex-patients could function better they sometimes became attendants. The recently mad knew all about coping with madness.

These developments inspired William Tuke to start a radical new type of institution in northern England, following the death of a fellow Quaker in a local asylum in 1790. In 1796, he founded the York Retreat, where 30 patients lived as part of a small community in a quiet country house where they were encouraged to rest, talk

DOI: 10.4324/9780429344664-2

and perform manual labour. There were few restraints. Tuke believed such moral treatment would make them calmer and more rational.

The York Retreat inspired similar institutions in the United States, like the Hartford Retreat which is still working under a name which makes one to think of Voltaire's Pangloss who thought everything was for the best in the best of all possible worlds, the Institute of Living.

Psychobabble had nothing on this

The other development was one of those fads which sometimes sweeps through psychology – phrenology. Or the science of the bumps on the skull which 19th-century phrenologists trumpeted was "the only true science of mind." It stemmed from the theories of the Viennese physician Franz Joseph Gall (1758–1828). He claimed that:

1. The brain is the organ of the mind.
2. The mind is composed of multiple distinct, innate faculties.
3. Because they are distinct, each faculty must have a separate seat or "organ" in the brain.
4. The size of an organ, other things being equal, is a measure of its power.
5. The shape of the brain is determined by the development of the various organs.
6. As the skull takes its shape from the brain, the surface of the skull can be read as an accurate index of psychological aptitudes and tendencies.

For example, a prominent bump on the forehead at the position attributed to the organ of benevolence showed that the individual had a "well developed" organ of benevolence, and so would be marvellously benevolent. There were also bumps for secretiveness, amativeness and much else.

It was in America that phrenology found its most devoted and enduring audience. Johann Spurzheim expanded Gall's theory and adopted the name "phrenology," and crossed the Atlantic in 1832. He lectured at Harvard and Yale. Ralph Waldo Emerson described him as one of the world's greatest minds. After Spurzheim's death, a ministry student named Orson Fowler began to lecture at

Amherst College in Massachusetts, and to offer "readings" for 2 cents apiece. In the future Rev. Henry Ward Beecher, Fowler reported finding evidence of a "strong social brain" with "very large Benevolence."

Phrenology even made it into the law courts when a nine-year-old boy was accused of a serious assault in 1840. The defence argued the boy "had received an injury of the head, in the consequence of a fall while quite young, whereby the portion of the brain called, by Phrenologists, the organ of Destructiveness, was preternaturally enlarged and a destructive disposition excited." A blow to the head had left him with a permanent bump behind his right ear, supposed evidence of a permanently swollen appetite for destruction. Since a child is not responsible for falling on his head, the defence argued, neither is that child responsible for the consequences of falling on his head. And if the assault resulted from an earlier damage to his "organ of Destructiveness," then the boy could not be held legally responsible for that assault.

The judge was not impressed and ordered that all phrenological testimony be thrown out. "Where people do not speak from knowledge, we cannot suffer a mere theory to go as evidence to a jury," he warned. The boy was found guilty and sentenced to nine years of hard labour.

Nevertheless, America quickly became cranium-conscious. Employers advertised for workers with particular phrenological profiles. Women began changing their hairstyles to show off their more flattering phrenological features. The rich and famous and many others queued to be felt up, as it were, by the phrenologists. Predictably, P.T. Barnum who owned circuses scored high in all traits but "Cautiousness."

Orson Fowler churned out the *American Phrenological Journal and Miscellany* (which remained in print until 1911). His books on how phrenology made one healthier, happier, richer and a better parent sold very well. Fowler also printed the first volume by a young writer named Walt Whitman.

Emerson, after reading a manuscript of *Leaves of Grass*, wrote to Whitman, "I greet you at the beginning of a great career," and his letter was addressed in care of Fowler. In the book itself, the lure of phrenology is clear: "Who are you indeed who would talk or sing of America?" Whitman wrote. "Have you ... learn'd the ... phrenology ... of the land?" So pleased was Whitman with his own phrenological reading ("large hope and comparison ... and causality") that he quoted it time and time again in his writings. Charlotte Brontë's work is also laced with phrenological analyses.

In the 1840s, Queen Victoria and her husband Prince Albert were so worried about the behaviour of their eldest son, and they called in a phrenologist. After feeling the future king's skull, the verdict was the boy lacked moral sense and was lazy. Edward turned into a contradictory character – brave, randy, a risk taker (he challenged Winston Churchill's father to duel), but he also became a competent king. Edgar Allan Poe also regularly wove phrenological concepts into his work, using cranial descriptions in an 1850 series of sketches of New York literary figures.

When one attempts to trace the connection between psychology and detective writing, one must be prepared to bump up, as it were, against the unexpected. Poe, who was, as we have seen, interested in phrenology, was a true original. He was born in Boston in 1809. Both his parents were actors; his father was also an alcoholic. After losing both his parents and a sister, he was looked after by foster parents who made sure he had a good education. Poe went briefly to university and then joined the military, but he suffered from depression. His life interested Princess Marie Bonaparte, one of Freud's great friends. She wrote a 700-page psychobiography of Poe. His gothic stories – with the return to life of dead persons and the eerie, unexpected turns of events – fascinated her. Her fascination can be traced to the fact they both had traumatic childhoods. Bonaparte had lost her mother a month after her birth. Her father was a keen mountaineer and spent little time with her. Poe's father deserted the family when Poe was two years old, and his mother died of tuberculosis when he was three.

In 1840, Poe applied for a job as a cryptographer; he failed to get it, but he made use of the experience in his famous *The Murders in the Rue Morgue*. In a letter to his friend Dr. Joseph Snodgrass, Poe said "its theme was the exercise of ingenuity in detecting a murderer." As it is the original whodunnit, it is worth discussing it in a little detail.

In Paris in 1840, the narrator meets Auguste Dupin who has

a busy, forceful mind. This mind could, it seemed, look right through a man's body into his soul and uncover his deepest thoughts. Sometimes he seemed to be not one, but two people – one who coldly put things together, and another who just as coldly took them apart.

Dupin also is "fond of enigmas, of conundrums, hieroglyphics; exhibiting in his solutions of each a degree of *acumen* which appears to the ordinary apprehension preternatural." And, like Poe, he gloats about his superior powers of perception, boasting, "with a low chuckling laugh, that most men, in respect to himself, wore windows in their bosoms."

Dupin read of the killings on 7 July 1840 when neighbours heard cries of terror from a house in the Rue Morgue. Only Mrs. L'Espanaye and her daughter lived there. Several neighbours and a policeman rushed into the house and heard two voices. On the fourth floor, they found a locked door with the key inside. They forced it open and saw broken chairs and tables lying all around the room.

Poe wrote,

> There was blood everywhere, on the floor, on the bed, on the walls. A sharp knife covered with blood was lying on the floor. In front of the fireplace there was some long grey hair, also bloody; it seemed to have been pulled from a human head. On the floor were four pieces of gold, an earring, several objects made of silver, and two bags containing a large amount of money in gold.

Clothes had been flung around the room. They found the daughter's body by the fireplace.

There was blood on her face and dark, deep marks which seemed to have been made by strong fingers.

The witnesses found the body of the old woman outside. Her neck was almost cut through, and when they tried to lift her up, her head fell off.

Talking to the witnesses did not make things clearer or explain the mystery of the money found in the room. Jules Mignaud said that Mrs. L'Espanaye had an account in his bank, but three days before her death, she withdrew a large amount of money. It was scattered on the floor, so robbery could not have been the motive. Poe never explained why Mrs. L'Espayane had withdrawn the money.

The voices were most puzzling. A policeman, Isidore Muset, heard the voice of a foreigner. Alberto Montani said the screams had lasted for about two minutes. He thought both voices were French, but he could not understand any of the words they spoke.

In this tale, Poe invented the locked room mystery which became such a favourite of the genre. The windows were closed and firmly locked on the inside. There were no stairs the killer could have gone down while the witnesses were going into the house.

Poe then introduced his amateur detective Dupin. The man first arrested for the murders, Auguste Le Bon, once did him a favour, and so Dupin offers to help the Prefet of Police as he hopes to clear Le Bon.

As the witnesses cannot agree on the language of the voices, Dupin concludes they were not hearing human voices. He searches the house and works out that the murderer would have had to have superhuman strength to force the daughter's body up the chimney. Dupin then hits on the idea that the murderer could have climbed up a lightning rod on the outside of the building to get in. Dupin finds an unusual tuft of hair at the scene and makes an out-landish leap.

If Poe pioneered the locked room mystery, few writers have imitated the rest of the story. The tuft of hair is not human, Dupin concludes, so the killer cannot be either. He settles on an unlikely species, an ourang-outang, as the killer. Dupin then places an ad-vertisement in the Paris papers, asking if anyone has lost such an animal.

A sailor answers and explains that he captured an orang-outang in Borneo and brought it back to Paris. "Monkey do as monkey see" is the next leap in the story. The beast must have seen the sailor shaving and then tried to shave its own face. The sailor be-came furious; the ape fled into the streets and reached the Rue Morgue. There it climbed up the lightning rod into the house, Dupin decided.

The ape seized the mother by the hair and waved the razor, which it must somehow have grabbed from the sailor. When the mother screamed the enraged ape ripped her hair out, slashed her throat and strangled her daughter. The sailor climbed up the lightning rod to try to catch the animal, so the two voices witnesses heard belonged to the orang-outang and the sailor. No wonder no one could make out what was being said. Afraid the sailor would punish him, the ape threw the mother's body out of the window, stuffed the daughter's into the chimney and fled.

Once Dupin gives his solution, the sailor sells the orang-outang. Le Bon is released, and the Prefet of Police says people should mind their own business. Dupin comments that the Prefet is "somewhat too cunning to be profound." Poe then gave Dupin a line which has become well known. "When you eliminate the impossible, the improbable, however improbable it is, must be the truth." As a teenager, Conan Doyle read Poe avidly but then became critical of him.

That did not stop him filching the line about the improbable and putting it in the mouth of Sherlock Holmes, a filch Dorothy Sayers noticed in her *Strong Poison*. With good reason, Stephen King called all later detective writers "The children of Poe." For nearly 30 years no writer, however, followed in Poe's footsteps.

In Britain, though the issue of the sanity of a murderer became a topic of intense debate. Three years after Poe published the story, Daniel McNaughton was acquitted on the charge of murdering Edward Drummond. McNaughton had shot him thinking him to be the prime minister Robert Peel. There had also been an attempt to kill Queen Victoria herself, so Parliament took action. It passed the Lunacy Act of 1845 which created asylums which would treat the mentally ill with far more kindness than before.

In 1861, Broadmoor, the country's most famous asylum for the criminally insane, opened. The first patients included the painter Richard Dadd who had killed his father; he was given a studio to carry on his work. Impossible today! Another killer William Major was an American surgeon who contributed entries to the *Oxford Dictionary* without ever telling the editor he was in an asylum. *The Illustrated London News* devoted a large piece to the asylum whose inmates were encouraged to practice music, dancing and art to heal them. Harvey Gordon's history makes clear how psychiatrists studied, contained and sometimes helped murderers (Gordon 2012). Literature was less progressive, though, and still usually depicted the mentally ill as dangerous. In 1839, Charlotte Brontë visited a medieval manor house. She was fascinated by an attic passageway: behind a hidden door in the wall panelling, a secret staircase led to a small corner of the attic known as "Mad Mary's Room." Years ago, Mary had been locked in there by the rest of the family, either to protect her or to hide her in shame.

When she sat down to write *Jane Eyre* a few years later, Charlotte Brontë used this experience. Jane goes to work as a governess for the son of the rich Rochester. Rochester is drawn to Jane; she is fascinated by him. He has a secret though. He has imprisoned his wife in the attic. Bertha is both Creole and mad. When Jane discovers that Rochester has acted so cruelly she runs away from him. In the end, since the mad wife burns the house down, Jane realises Rochester had reasons for his actions. And Bronte added the famous line "Reader I married him." *Jane Eyre* was hugely successful as a book and as intertextual icon. She has not just been turned into a detective. In *Jane Steele*, a novel written in 2001, Jane Eyre features. She suffers at the hands of her aunt and schoolmaster. They call her wicked – but she fears the accusation is true. When she flees, she leaves behind the corpses of her tormentors. But did she kill them? Jane Eyre lives on in a variety of guises.

Writers found insanity tantalising. In 1861, Wilkie Collins published *The Moonstone* and then *The Woman in White*. The story centres on Laura, a young woman who is the woman in white; Anne Catherick. She was mentally disabled and was devoted to Laura's mother, who dressed her in white. Again, it is immediately clear who the villain is.

Laura marries the evil Sir Percival Glyde but refuses to sign away her fortune. Sir Percival and his assistant then decide to use the resemblance between Laura and Anne. They trick the two women into travelling to London, Laura will be placed in an asylum under Anne's name and Anne will be buried as Laura when she dies which is expected to be soon. So Glyde will get his hands on Laura's loot. The plan does not quite work and ends in another all-consuming fire when Glyde tries to burn incriminating documents; he dies in the flames.

Collins' more obscure *The Law and the Lady* is interesting as it provides the first woman detective. On Valeria's wedding day a letter from her uncle warns her against her husband, who encourages her to leave him without explaining why she should do that.

"We must part my angel," Eustace says, "how can you marry a man who is the object of suspicion to your nearest and dearest friends?" He begs her for one last kiss and asks her to forgive him for having loved her.

"I held him desperately, recklessly," Valeria said as "his words filled me with a frenzy of despair." She did not care what her friends might hint at. "I can't live without you. I must and will be your wife."

Valeria then discovers her husband has changed his name and was tried for murdering his first wife. The verdict was not proven, which did not really clear him. She sets out to prove to herself and the world that he was innocent and eventually discovers the real killer, a woman. Mrs. Beaufy was jealous of Eustace's first wife and poisoned her.

Twenty-four centuries after Aristotle, psychology took a great leap forward towards becoming a science when two eminent Victorians rose from their armchairs and set up laboratories.

Chapter 3

The birth of modern psychology

1879 and the significance of apparently unconnected events

In 1879 the American William James and the German Wilhelm Wundt established the first psychological laboratories ever. They were at Harvard and in Leipzig. Wundt wanted to identify the atoms of the mind just as physicists were identifying the atoms of matter.

In 1879 Sigmund Freud, who was 23 years old, was a medical student at the University of Vienna, and doing research on the reproduction of eels. Eels did not really capture his imagination, and he went on to study the unconscious, which led him eventually to his own self-analysis and to the creation of psychoanalysis.

In 1879 Arthur Conan Doyle was studying medicine at Edinburgh University and began writing short stories. On 20 September 1879, he published his first academic article, "Gelsemium as a Poison," in the *British Medical Journal*. The *Daily Telegraph* saw this study as potentially useful in murder investigations. Conan Doyle outlined his use of a tincture of gelseminum for treating a case of neuralgia, or neuropathic (nerve) pain. The 19-year-old was "determined to ascertain how far one might go in taking the drug, and what the primary symptoms of an overdose might be."

Conan Doyle prepared a fresh tincture, noted the dose and physiological effects, avoided tobacco and dosed himself at the same time each day.

At low doses of 40 and 60 minums (1 minum = 1 drop = 0.06 mL) he observed no effects, but 20 minutes after ingesting 90 minums he experienced extreme "giddiness." At 120 minums the giddiness was less, but several hours later he had problems seeing. Psychological symptoms disappeared by 150 minums, and all that remained were headaches and diarrhoea. Doyle pushed on

DOI: 10.4324/9780429344664-3

towards 200 minum, at which persistent diarrhoea, headache and weak pulse got the better of him.

Conan Doyle concluded that healthy adults could take up to 90 minums, but that doses of 90–120 would lead to the drug-induced mild paralysis. Higher doses caused worst side effects, but he believed a person could tolerate them. He signed off the letter with the bravado and gravitas we would expect from a man with a bit of Sherlock Holmes in him:

> I feel convinced that I could have taken as much as half an ounce of the tincture, had it not been for the extreme diarrhoea it brought on.

In 1879 too, the German psychiatrist Richard Krafft Ebbing was working on his book *Psychopathis Sexualis* whose details were so shocking the book eventually had to be published in Latin. It contained a very early case history of what we now call a serial killer.

By 1879 there were some 1200 railway stations in the United Kingdom. Most had bookstalls as passengers needed something to help them pass the time while they travelled. W.H. Smith set up the first railway station bookstall at Euston Station in 1848.

By 1879 W.H. Smith dominated the bookstall trade, had entered politics as a Tory and later became a cabinet minister. Six years later he had a fierce battle with Lord Randolph Churchill, Winston Churchill's father, over defence spending.

Winston Churchill suffered from what he called "the black dog." He was always suspicious of psychiatry, and thought painting was a far better therapy when he was depressed. I have argued elsewhere he did not suffer from depression but manic depression.

Both Agatha Christie and Winston Churchill were frequent visitors to the Old Cataract Hotel in Aswan in Egypt, where Christie was inspired to write *Death on the Nile*. Both have suites in the hotel named after them.

Churchill wrote a political thriller in his 20s but did not try fiction again till 1946 when he wrote *The Dream*, a story which has a familiar detective theme; characters re-appear from the past, and family secrets are dangerous. In *The Dream* his long-dead father appears to Churchill in his studio at his country house at Chartwell. Churchill's demanding and disappointed father was pleased to see his son was at least comfortably off. He asks him what he had done in his career.

He was in the army, Winston replies. True but hardly the whole truth.

What rank, his father asks. A Major. Hardly glorious, but such a middling rank would have suited the son he always thought unimpressive.

The son who disappointed his father does not want to hurt him even if he is a ghost. So Churchill says little about either his military or political career. In fact he became First Lord of the Admiralty and, in 1940, prime minister, the office his father always thought he himself deserved.

Then Churchill saved the world with the help of Clement Attlee. Attlee was interested in psychoanalysis; his friend James Strachey translated Freud into English.

Hunt the thimble

Freud once called psychoanalysis a game like hunt the thimble. Both the detective and the analyst seek hidden truths – and the two have sometimes been compared. As he unpicked dreams, memories, fantasies and associations, Freud probed the unconscious of his patients who resisted and denied, just as suspects often do in police stations. One of his patients the poet Hilda Doolittle wrote *A Tribute to Freud*.

Freud told her did not just compare analysis to hunt the thimble, but later added that it was like doing a jigsaw. The detective is doing exactly the same, and his thimble is, in its way, as complicated. That thimble has three parts – who did it, why and how.

When he hunted the thimble, Holmes often used a microscope as Freud did in his early work on eels. Holmes relied on the best microscopes and magnifying glasses of the 1890s according to one of the many Holmesian scholars. In his paper "The Art of Forensic Detection and Sherlock Holmes," Ing deduced that Holmes would have usually used a "10 power silver and chrome magnifying glass, a brass tripod base monocular optical microscope probably manufactured by Powell and Lealand. Watson dutifully recorded Holmes's use of the magnifying glass:

> As he spoke, he whipped a tape measure and a large round magnifying glass from his pocket. With these two implements he trotted noiselessly about the room, sometimes stopping, occasionally kneeling, and once lying flat upon his face. ... As I

watched him I was irresistibly reminded of a pure-blooded well-trained foxhound as it dashes backwards and forwards through the covert, whining in its eagerness, until it comes across the lost scent.

No one ever compared Freud to a foxhound but he too liked to ferret out secrets. Unlike some of his contemporaries though Freud did not believe in religious revelations.

Chapter 4

Psychology and mystical experiences

The late 19th century and the work of William James and Conan Doyle, allies in the mystical

As psychology became more of experimental science in the 1880s and 1890s, some scientists became interested in exploring the inexplicable.

William James had begun teaching at Harvard in 1872. Mystical experiences interested him all his life. He experimented with substances including nitrous oxide and peyote. Only when he was under the influence of nitrous oxide, he said, did he manage to understand Hegel's philosophy. Since nitrous oxide makes one laugh, this suggests he did not take Hegel too seriously. Nevertheless, James concluded that while the revelations of the mystic may be true, they may be true only for the mystic. You needed personal experience to have any real sense of them. Mystical experiences were passive. Mystics felt controlled by a superior power. Words really failed because language could not properly describe the experience. He used the word "noetic" because the "truths" that were revealed to mystics were utterly special.

The link between Conan Doyle and William James was very much a product of their time. James became president of the Society for Psychical Research, and Conan Doyle was an important member until 1918. The Society attracted many famous scientists including the chemist Sir William Crooker, the physicist Sir Oliver Lodge and the Nobel laureate Charles Richet. At the same time, as Freud Richet was an intern at the Salpêtrière Hospital in Paris, he observed Charcot's work with then so-called hysterical patients. Richet won the Nobel Prize for his work on anaphylaxis, the term he coined for an individual's sometimes-lethal reaction to a second, small injection. Richet's research helped understand hay fever,

DOI: 10.4324/9780429344664-4

asthma and other allergic reactions. He also wrote at least one detective story, *Sister Marthe*.

The Society for Psychical Research exposed some fake mediums, alleged apparitions of ectoplasm and studied hypnotism, the transference of thoughts and the Reichenbach phenomena – it was no accident Conan Doyle set his famous scene with Holmes and Moriarty at the Reichenbach Falls. The phenomenon was said to be an energy field emanating from crystals, magnets and living things. The Austrian chemist and metallurgist Baron Karl von Reichenbach (1788–1869) identified it and held it to be a manifestation of an all-pervading physical force that he named Od or Odyle after the Norse god Odin.

The Society also carried out the *Census of Hallucinations* in 1894 which sampled 17,000 people. Out of these, 1,684 reported having experienced a hallucination or an apparition.

In his *Gifford Lectures* at Edinburgh, James offered a wide-ranging account of the varieties of religious experiences. He claimed:

- Religious experience should be the primary topic in the study of religion, rather than religious institutions.
- Psychologists should seek out intense, even pathological varieties of experience (religious or otherwise) because they represent the closest thing to a microscope of the mind. They showed us in drastically enlarged form the normal processes of things.
- A variety of characteristics can be seen within a single individual. There are subconscious elements that compose the scattered fragments of a personality.
- Religious Mysticism is only one half of mysticism; the other half is composed of the insane and both of these are co-located in the "great subliminal or transmarginal region."

James' study was hugely influential for decades. In 1974, I interviewed Sir Alistair Hardy, a conventional marine biologist whose studies of plankton were important. He also gathered newspaper accounts of religious experiences as, among much else, he wanted to see how right James had been.

James too studied more conventional topics. His theory of emotions is a classic, which is interesting in terms of serial killers. He argued an emotion started with an arousing stimulus and ended with a passionate feeling, a conscious emotional experience. James asked: "do we run from a bear because we are afraid or are we afraid because we run?" To him the obvious answer that we run because we are afraid was wrong. We are afraid because we run. My theory, on the contrary, is that the bodily changes follow directly the perception of the exciting fact and that our feeling of the same changes as they occur IS the emotion.

James argued that emotions are often accompanied by bodily responses (racing heart, tight stomach, sweaty palms, tense muscles, and that we can sense what is going on inside our body in much the same way as we can sense what is going on in the outside world. Emotions feel different from other states of mind because they have these bodily responses that give rise to internal sensations, and different emotions feel different from one another because they are accompanied by different bodily responses and sensations. For example, when we see a bear, we run away. During our escape, the body goes into physiological overdrive: blood pressure rises, heart rate increases, pupils dilate, palms sweat, muscles contract. Other emotional situations will result in different bodily upheavals. In each case, the physiological responses return to the brain in the form of bodily sensations, and the unique pattern of sensory feedback gives each emotion its unique quality. Fear feels different from anger or love because it has a different physiological signature. Feelings are the slaves of physiology, not vice versa: we do not tremble because we are afraid or cry because we feel sad; we are afraid because we tremble and are sad because we cry. The serial killer often is excited physiologically as he or she contemplates killing, but his or her responses often lead not to anxiety but calm.

When James published his theory of emotions in 1884, Conan Doyle began to work on Sherlock Holmes. He made his sleuth into a supreme reasoning machine who scrutinised footprints, bloodstains and often mud on shoes which showed where a person had been.

Freud was sceptical about religions, but he and James shared an interest in "substances." In his novel *The Seven-Per-Cent Solution*, Nicholas Meyer even teamed Freud with Holmes. The 7% solution is the cocaine both men were addicted to. Freud took it to calm his anxieties. When he was studying under the "Napoleon of neurosis," Jean Marie Charcot at the Salpêtrière Hospital in Paris, the young Freud was sometimes invited to glittering salons. He was unsure of himself and took cocaine to brave himself up. Holmes never needed more social confidence but took the drug when he was bored due to the failure of the criminal classes to provide him with interesting cases.

Contradictions

Any study of detective fiction soon hits contradictions. There is no *Journal of Poirot Studies*, while there are at least 40,000 books and papers on Holmes including much psychiatric literature. The *Bulletin of the Menninger Clinic* even published a long paper which psychoanalysed Holmes.

Holmes inspires obsession. Dorothy Sayers in five essays collected in *Unpopular Opinions* devoted one to the vital question of whether Holmes went to Oxford or Cambridge and what he might have studied. Another essay is devoted to Watson's marriage and the effect it had on Holmes. Sayers provides far more background on Holmes than Conan Doyle ever did. Guilt made Conan Doyle's reticent about Holmes' childhood.

Freud said his mother's love made him feel like "a conquistador," giving him self-confidence. Adam Philipps in *Becoming Freud* points out that we know very little, in fact, about Freud's confidence-giving mother. Conan Doyle's mother was also a major positive influence. She loved books and was a good storyteller. She knew how to lower "her voice to a horror-stricken whisper" when she reached the climax of a story. "In my early childhood, as far as I can remember anything at all, the vivid stories she would tell me stand out so clearly that they obscure the real facts of my life."

Both men had to cope with fathers who were failures. Freud's father was a businessman who went bankrupt at least once, while Conan Doyle's father was an alcoholic. In order to spare him too much contact with his chaotic father, an uncle paid for Conan Doyle to be sent to a Jesuit boarding school when he was eight. He disliked it but discovered he had a talent for storytelling. Years later he wrote,

> Perhaps it was good for me that the times were hard, for I was wild, full-blooded and a trifle reckless. But the situation called for energy and application so that one was bound to try to meet it. My mother had been so splendid that I could not fail her.

Freud also faced a family crisis when he was young. When he was ten he was devastated because his uncle Joseph was sent to jail for forging Russian roubles. That memory made him frame his theories in such a way they were hard to falsify. The parallel between a false theory and forgery is not hard to grasp.

Freud was canny and careful in choosing Ernest Jones as his biographer because Jones was utterly loyal to him. Conan Doyle did not encourage any biographers – and for one reason above all. He first encountered psychiatrists when he had to co-sign the committal papers of his father, who by then was seriously demented as a result of his excessive drinking. The dramatic circumstances which surrounded the confinement of his father to a lunatic asylum influenced *The Surgeon of Gaster Fell*, a story published in four instalments.

The unnamed narrator rents an isolated cottage and meets an entrancing woman. Eva says she can never marry but refuses to explain why. The narrator's neighbour is aggressive. It turns out he is keeping an old man prisoner in his house. Eventually, we discover the old man is his father who was once a respectable doctor. Eva fears that if she married and had a child, that child would also end up mad.

Turning your trauma into a story is, of course, a way of trying to control the trauma because you control the tale. In his biography, Stashower (1999) dissects the difficult relationship between Conan Doyle and his father, Charles. Charles called his condition "the dreadful secret"; at the time seeming respectable was vital. Conan Doyle did little to help his father in the 1890s after he became rich and famous. He went so far as to lie, claiming his father died while he was still not well known when, in fact, his father died years later. Stashower argues that even 30 years after his father died "his son did not wish to invite undue interest" in the man.

The model for Holmes

The man who influenced Conan Doyle's work most was one of his teachers in the medical school at Edinburgh, Dr. Joseph Bell. Bell was a master at observation, logic, deduction and diagnosis, and became the model for Sherlock Holmes. Conan Doyle in his autobiography gave many examples of Bell's methods. Bell would gather his students and a man he had never seen before in the lecture theatre.

"A cobbler I see," Bell said. He then explained to the students that the inside of the man's trousers was worn at the knee where the man rested his lapstone or sharpening tool. Conan Doyle then gave a second example.

A patient was shown at the outpatients' clinic. Before the patient can say a word, Bell says.

"Well my man I see you've served in the army."
"Aye sir." The man would turn out to be a man of few words.
"Not long discharged?"
"Aye sir."
"A Highland regiment?"
"Aye sir."
"A non commissioned officer?"
"Aye sir."
"Stationed at Barbados?"
"Aye sir"

Bell then turned to his students and explained how he had arrived at his conclusions:

You see gentleman, the patient is a respectful man, but he did not remove his hat. They do not do this in the army. He would have learned this civilian habit had he been long discharged. He has an air of authority and he is obviously Scottish. As to Barbados, his complaint is elephantiasis which could be West Indian but not European.

Impressed Conan Doyle wrote a very similar exchange when Holmes and his brother Mycroft looked out of the Diogenes Club and observed a man in the street which led to a spate of deductions.

Bell was not entirely delighted, however, when Conan Doyle gave an interview singling him out as the model for Sherlock. He complained the Holmes stories were a "cataract of drivel" and resented the fact that he was connected with "such a heap of rubbish."

The observation of the physical

In 1888, Sherlock Holmes' third adventure was published in *Beeton's Christmas Annual* as *A Study in Scarlet*. It offers the first double act of smart detective and not-so-smart sidekick, Sherlock Holmes and Dr. Watson.

Ing, an expert on Holmes, argues Holmes was well versed in forensic science before there was a forensic science to be well versed in. In *A Study in Scarlet*, Watson claims Holmes' knowledge of botany is "variable," his skill in geography is "practical but limited," his knowledge of chemistry "profound" and his knowledge of human anatomy "accurate." He needed them all to make "the science of deduction" possible. Ing has closely read the four Sherlock novels and the 56 stories and echoes Watson. Holmes, Ing lists, has a working knowledge of chemistry, bloodstain identification, botany, geology, anatomy, law, cryptanalysis, fingerprinting, document examination, ballistics and forensic medicine.

The way Holmes displayed his talents sometimes was like a bright child showing off; he cannot resist, for example, when Watson has just returned to 221a Baker St. He riffs: "How do I know that you have been getting yourself very wet lately, and that you have a most clumsy and careless servant girl?" Holmes "chuckled to himself and rubbed his long, nervous hands together." It was elementary as usual. The leather of Watson's left shoe which was muddy "is scored by six almost parallel cuts." The mud showed Watson had been out in vile weather and the fact that it had not been scraped properly suggested his servant girl was slapdash. To cap it all Holmes slammed in:

> Only a fool would fail to deduce that a man who smelt of iodoform and had a black mark of nitrate of silver on his right finger, and a bulge on the right side of his top-hat where he stashes his stethoscope, is not a doctor.

Holmes would not have been so interesting if he had just been a human reasoning machine. Conan Doyle also gave him psychological flaws – arrogance, mood swings and lassitude when there were no cases to solve. He also made him a good violinist. Cocaine and music helped with his depressions. Watson tried to offer him help with his mood swings, which did not please his friend.

Freud argued the mind censored itself so as not to be conscious of unbearable pain. His father tried hard to mend their sometimes-fractured relationship before he died in 1896. Freud, however, felt his father's death as a liberation, and that same year, he started on his own self-analysis, which led to his development of psychoanalysis. Conan Doyle never managed to free himself. It is no accident that he never made Holmes probe psychiatric issues in any depth; he did not want to explore these and censored himself because his father had been so disturbed and disturbing. The memories would have been too painful. Freud would have seen this as a rather crude defence mechanism.

A scandal in Bohemia

Detail, detail and more detail suggest obsession. In *A Scandal in Bohemia,* Holmes hands Watson an unsigned note which announced a masked man would call and immediately produces a cascade of deductions.

> "The 'G' with the small 't' stands for 'Gesellschaft,' which is the German for 'Company' ... 'P,' of course, stands for 'Papier.' Now for the 'Eg.' Let us glance at our Continental Gazetteer." The book gives a clue. Ha, ha, my boy, what do you make of that?" His eyes sparkled, and he sent up a great blue triumphant cloud from his cigarette. "The paper was made in Bohemia," Holmes finished.

They stop talking when a tall man arrives, wearing a mask, of course. "You may address me as the Count von Kramm, a Bohemian nobleman," the masked man barks. The Count demands absolute secrecy as what he is about to tell them "may have an influence upon European history."

The mask is not much of a mask for Holmes who slices through the Bohemian's disguise at once. The man shouts: "You are right," he cried; "I am the King. Why should I attempt to conceal it?"

The King is about to be married to a respectable princess, but he had an affair with Irene Adler, an opera singer. He wrote her passionate letters and took a photograph of the two of them together. He is afraid she may use these to stop his marriage.

Holmes and Watson then go to Adler's house. Holmes has arranged for some men to start a fight outside, and he protects Adler who invites him inside. Watson tosses in a smoke rocket. While smoke billows out of the building, Watson shouts "FIRE!" As Holmes expected, Adler rushes to save her most precious possession – the photograph of herself and the king. Holmes sees it is kept in a recess behind a sliding panel.

When Holmes, Watson and the king arrive at Adler's house at 8 a.m. the next morning, her elderly maid informs them Madame has left the country by train. Holmes goes to the hiding place, where he finds a photograph of Adler and a letter to him. In it, Adler tells Holmes she has left England with "a better man" than the king. She promises not to compromise him, however.

Holmes takes the photograph of Adler as a memento; she is the only woman who attracts him, which raises the question of how much he felt for Watson. Some commentators have suggested they had an unspoken and never acted upon homosexual attraction. Certainly, their relationship cooled once Watson married. *In Bed with Sherlock Holmes* is entirely devoted to Holmes' sex life which is rather restricted.

Psychoanalytic re-interpretations

In terms of the history of psychology, two books are especially interesting. *Durkheim Is Dead!: A Sherlock Holmes Mystery of Social Theory* is as much about high jinks as about high scholarship. In 1910, the greatest social theorists in the world gather in London to discuss the new science of sociology. The social theorists are not model citizens; they fight; one steals a jewel, and the "father of sociology," Emile Durkheim disappears. As Holmes and Watson investigate, they get a grounding in social theory from its masters who include W. E. B. Du Bois, Freud, Lenin and Max Weber. Whodunnit meets textbook is a promising genre.

The most extreme critic of Holmes is Pierre Bayard. In *Sherlock Holmes Was Wrong: Re-opening the Case of the "Hound of the Baskervilles,"* he argues that Holmes got it wrong for a variety of reasons. Bayard writes: "Fictional characters are not, as often believed, beings of paper, but living creatures, who lead an autonomous life within the text and go as far as commit murder without the author's knowledge."

Bayard begins with pedestrian exposition of the plot which helps expose the shoddiness of Holmes' deductions and the improbability of the supposed solution. She asks why would a writer as brilliant as Conan Doyle make his detective commit such a gross blunder?

It has been suggested that Bayard seized on the fact that Conan Doyle had come to hate his most famous character. His publisher wanted more and more Holmes stories. Conan Doyle reluctantly relented, and thus wrote *The Hound of the Baskervilles*. There were queues waiting to buy the next instalment. Fools, according to Bayard. He argues that in settling on Jack Stapleton and his hound, Holmes nailed the wrong suspect.

Bayard highlights a number of problems: Why did the hound leave no marks on the first corpse, that of Sir Charles Baskerville? When Seldon, the convict, dies wearing Baskerville's clothes, the hound is never actually seen, so why assume that it was responsible? It does attack Sir Henry near the end, but only after a shot has wounded it first. Bayard also notes that, after deciding on Stapleton as his suspect, reading all the clues as pointing in his direction and then driving the man out onto the moor to his certain death, Holmes dismisses the issue of motive. When Watson questions him, Holmes admits this is "a formidable difficulty," but adds, "I fear you ask too much when you expect me to solve it."

Some critics do not accept Bayard's conclusion that Conan Doyle subconsciously set up Holmes to fail. They point out that Bayard is rather too inclined to attribute unconscious motives. In some opinion, Conan Doyle knew what he was doing perfectly well. His dislike of Holmes was perfectly conscious, and he enjoyed the idea of Holmes putting forward an absurd solution. To which one might few readers have complained about it.

Conan Doyle never let Holmes resolve his contradictions – the man of reason who needed drugs and was prone to depression – but that probably made Holmes more fascinating to readers.

The end of Holmes

Conan Doyle brought him back one last time in *The Adventure of the Empty House*. At the start of the story, Watson is alone. His wife is dead, and he believes Holmes to be dead as well. Then Watson has a surprise which, for once, has nothing to do with deductions he failed to make.

> I moved my head to look at the cabinet behind me. When I turned again, Sherlock Holmes was standing smiling at me across my study table. I rose to my feet, stared at him for some seconds in utter amazement, and then it appears that I must have fainted for the first and the last time in my life. Certainly, a grey mist swirled before my eyes, and when it cleared I found my collar-ends undone and the tingling after-taste of brandy

upon my lips. Holmes was bending over my chair, his flask in
his hand.

Holmes explains he had been wandering the world after defeating
Moriarty at the Reichenbach Falls. He spent two years in Tibet
where he met the "head lama," then to Persia and Mecca. Finally,
he did chemical research on coal tar derivatives in Montpellier, no
doubt using the best microscopes France could provide. Such work
was hardly psychological.

Holmes and Watson then go to their old apartment in Baker
Street, where Holmes' rooms had been kept for him. With Watson
now a widower, they resume the life they started on together 17
years earlier.

This chapter started by asking why some authors come to hate
their detectives. Conan Doyle was exasperated that the success of
Sherlock made critics pay less attention to his other work, especially the historical novels that he thought were much better. There
was another reason, as I have argued. He created Sherlock at a time
when he was distressed about his father's alcoholism which he had
to keep secret. Repression was the reason; Conan Doyle felt guilty.
The success of the Holmes stories reminded him of how much he
had ignored his father and that disturbed him. Conan Doyle became very interested in the supernatural and contacting the dead,
though he never admitted that might be linked to his guilt towards
his father. One could speculate that he hoped that, maybe from
beyond the grave, his father might forgive him.

When Conan Doyle and James were writing, psychology saw a
new theory that helps explain our fascination with the detective
genre as it explains our love of patterns.

Chapter 5

Puzzles, riddles and Gestalt theory

The early 20th century and the work of G.K. Chesterton

In *The Idea of the Brain* (2020), Matthew Cobb argues how little we still know of how the brain works. He compares the human brain with those of lobsters that manage with only 33 neurons as opposed to the billions we enjoy.

Our failure to understand the lobster's brain shows that despite advances in imaging we are far from grasping how the human brain manages to think. One certainty is that the human brain likes puzzles and the resolution of puzzles. There is no evidence lobsters do. We don't have to understand neurophysiology to appreciate why our love of puzzles helps explain our love of detective stories. Dorothy Sayers argued a good one was like a puzzle whose solution surprised readers but did not leave them feeling cheated; they had been offered all the clues needed to solve it but failed to do so.

Sayers once compared solving a mystery to getting an anagram. She gave COSSSSRI as an example of a small Eureka moment where "by no logical process the conscious mind can detect" the solution SCISSORS "presents itself with calm certainty." She also contrasted two approaches to solving crimes – rational deduction, where clues lead to the culprit, and the intuitive leap.

Intuition brings us to the dramatic moment in Tolkein's *The Hobbit,* upon which everything else turns. Bilbo finds a ring deep in a cave in the mountains. Gollum, the owner of the "precious" as he calls it, is desperate to get it back. Neither of them knows it is a ring of power which has been lost for generations. To recover it, Gollum challenges Bilbo to solve a riddle.

What has roots as nobody sees,
Is taller than trees,

DOI: 10.4324/9780429344664-5

Up, up it goes,
And yet never grows?

When Bilbo gives the right answer – mountains – Gollum insists he cheated and demands another chance to defeat him. The next riddle is:

Voiceless cries
Wingless flutters
Toothless bites
Mouthless mutters

Wind, Bilbo solves again. He gets the third riddle too and wins the ring, not knowing its power.

The riddle is, of course, a puzzle. And you can usually only solve the puzzle or whodunnit when the pattern falls into place.

In 1914, Tolkien fought in the First World War when a new theory of psychology was being developed, a theory that highlighted the brain's need for patterns: Gestalt theory; gestalt is German for pattern. Gestalt psychologists believed the search for such atoms missed the point. The principle behind their movement was that the whole was greater than the sum of its parts.

"The fundamental 'formula' of Gestalt theory might be expressed in this way," Max Wertheimer, the Czech psychologist, wrote:

There are wholes, the behaviour of which is not determined by that of their individual elements, but where the part-processes are themselves determined by the intrinsic nature of the whole. It is the hope of Gestalt theory to determine the nature of such wholes.

One day in 1910 at a train station, Wertheimer purchased a toy stroboscope, an instrument used to make an object appear to be moving as it produces brief repetitive flashes of light in rapid sequence. This is the principle on which the cinema works; a succession of still frames are seen as moving images. Our brains fill in the gaps so that we see a flow of movement.

The Gestalt movement also argued that when one stopped seeing parts and saw the whole, there was an unconscious leap in thinking that short-circuited normal reasoning. Many psychologists contest the value of Gestalt theory, but it helps explain why the solution of a detective novel gives us a feeling of satisfaction.

Wertheimer insisted that the "gestalt" is primary. He took the radical position that "what is given me by the melody does not arise ... as a secondary process from the sum of the pieces as such. Instead, what takes place in each single part already depends upon what the whole is" (1925/1938). In other words, one hears the melody first and only then may perceptually divide it up into notes. Similarly, in vision, one sees the form of the circle first – it is given "immediately." Only after this primary apprehension might one notice that it is made up of lines or dots or stars.

For the Gestalt psychologists, stimuli were said to have a certain structure to be organised in a certain way, and we respond to this structural organisation, rather than to individual sensory elements.

In 1921, Wertheimer's pupil Koffka published a Gestalt-oriented text on developmental psychology, *The Growth of the Mind*. A year later he introduced Gestalt theory to America in a paper in *Psychological Bulletin*. It voiced criticisms of then-current explanations of a number of problems of perception, and the alternatives offered by the Gestalt school. In 1935, Koffka published his *Principles of Gestalt Psychology*, which laid out the *Gestalt* vision of the scientific enterprise as a whole. Science, he said, is not the simple accumulation of facts. What makes research scientific is the incorporation of facts into a theoretical structure. The goal of the Gestalt movement was to integrate the facts of inanimate nature, life and mind into a single scientific structure. Science would have to accommodate not only what Koffka called the quantitative facts of physical science but the facts of two other "scientific categories": questions of order and questions of *Sinn*, a German word which has been variously translated as significance, value and meaning. Without incorporating the meaning of experience and behaviour, Koffka believed that science would doom itself to trivialities in studying human beings.

It is not hard to see why a species that likes to complete patterns would like whodunnits. Once you know the who, the why and how, the pattern is complete, the brain is replete.

Latest work on the puzzling brain

Recent neurological research at Ohio University has examined how the brain functions when seeing patterns and how that is different from the way the brain handles probabilistic learning. The Ohio researchers showed subjects 50 series of 12 images that included various combinations of three photos – a hand, a face and a landscape – sometimes in a pattern and sometimes in a random order. Participants were in an MRI machine that showed what parts of their brain were active as they chose what photo they thought was coming up next.

"We could see what parts of the brain were activated when participants figured out that there was a pattern – or realized that there was no pattern," according to Ian Krajbich, co-author of the study.

Humans try to detect patterns in their environment all the time because it makes learning easier. For example, if you are given driving directions in an unfamiliar city, you can try to memorise each turn. But if you see a pattern – for example, turn left, then right, then left, then right – it will be easier to remember.

"We realized that not much was known about how humans figure out these rules," the Ohio team wrote. Their study involved 26 adults. Each photo they were shown began as a scrambled image that became clear in three seconds. Subjects hit a button as soon as they thought they knew which one of the three images was being presented. The object was to select which image was being shown as quickly as possible.

"If they don't know what image is coming next, they have to wait a while and that is costing them money," according to Krajbich. "But once they figured out a pattern, they responded more quickly, and we could see how that was reflected in their brains."

"People in our study aren't just predicting the odds of which photo will show up next. They are learning patterns and developing rules that guide their decision and make them faster and more accurate," his colleague Igor Konovalov added.

Probabilistic and pattern learning differ in how they engage the brain. The researchers found different parts of the brain were active depending on which kind of uncertainty that the participants faced. As the participants worked out this question, a different part of the brain – the ventromedial prefrontal cortex – was activated. This part of the brain has been shown to be associated with reward. The hippocampus also was particularly active when participants were figuring out patterns. Subjects who had more hippocampal activity were faster learners.

"One interpretation is that people may be getting a sense of re-ward for figuring out whether there is a pattern or not. We don't know that for sure yet, but it is plausible," Krajbich said. He added, "The brain is keeping track of more things than we pre-viously thought. It isn't just about predicting what is coming next. It is looking for rules to help predict better and faster."

Riddles, like the ones Bilbo solves, are a type of puzzle and have much history. The Bible has riddles of which the first is Samson's. At his wedding feast, he confounded the Philistines: with a nifty conundrum. "Out of the eater came forth meat, and out of the strong came forth sweetness." The answer was honey from a lion's carcass, where bees had made a hive. An oddity indeed.

A thousand years later the mystical Muslim sect, the Sufis used riddles in teaching their philosophy. *The Tales of the Mullah Nasruddin* illustrates the profound meanings of jokes. A neighbour asked Nasruddin if he could borrow his donkey. Nasruddin did not want to and told him, "The donkey sadly is not here." He dis-appointed the neighbour and walked away but then, Mullah Nasruddin's donkey, which was in the back of his house all the time, let out a big bray. The neighbour complained, "Mullah Sahib, I thought you told me that your donkey was not here." Mullah Nasruddin replied, "My friend, who are you going to believe? Me or the donkey?"

Apes laugh, but humans laugh at far more

One of Britain's longest-serving puzzle setters is Chris Maslanka. His *Two Thousand Years of Puzzling* traced the history of hu-mankind's seemingly insatiable delight in puzzles and riddles. Maslanka shows how in the 19th century, the middle class had enough leisure to grow puzzling into a business. Masterman (2001) in *The Condition of England* blamed middle-class apathy and avarice for the puzzle craze. Avarice because papers often offered prizes. Dorothy Sayers included crossword puzzles in a number of her books.

Puzzles are obviously popular, or they would not feature so much in newspapers, magazines, TV and the Internet. Every day *The Times* carries its crossword so beloved of Colin Dexter's Inspector Morse, as well as the easier Quick Cryptic and the Times 2 Crossword for those who are anagram challenged. The paper also offers three Sudokus, the difficult, the fiendish and the super fiendish. Readers can also test their brains with three mental arithmetic puzzles as well as a Suko, a Polygon, the Train Tracks, a Lexica and a Codeword puzzle. You could spend three hours doing a lot before turning to the daily 15 general knowledge questions which demand knowledge of anything and everything from historical hit records to the paintings of Rembrandt. The less-highbrow *Evening Standard* offers nearly as many test your neurons games.

You don't have to play alone either in normal times. Most pubs run quiz nights, and The Grapes in Limehouse sometimes has Gandalf – yes he – asking the questions as Sir Ian McKellen is one of the pub's owners and sometimes joins one of the teams.

Jokes offer another example of our love of completing a pattern, for the punch line is closure. They are as old as the pyramids according to a team at the University of Wolverhampton. Its researchers claim that the world's oldest recorded joke dates back to 1900 B.C., and Freud would not have been surprised it was a dirty one. It went: "Something which has never occurred since time immemorial; a young woman did not fart in her husband's lap."

An Egyptian joke dating from 1600 B.C. is more even explicitly sexual and concerns a Pharaoh with a roving eye. It ran:

How do you entertain a bored Pharaoh? You sail a boatload of young women dressed only in fishing nets down the Nile and urge the pharaoh to go catch a fish.

In his *Jokes and Their Relation to the Unconscious*, Freud argued that a good punch line is satisfying because of what he called "psychic economy." The punch line neatly resolves the uncertainties the joke poses – and so resolves the psychological tension which that uncertainty provokes. In other words, it completes the pattern, just as the solution to a detective novel does.

Freud offered a formidable number of jokes to make the point. One nice one, an Italian lady revenged herself for a tactless remark made by Napoleon. At a court ball, he said to her, pointing to her fellow countrymen: "Tu tti gli Italiani danzano si male" [All Italians dance badly]. The lady replied, "Non tutti, ma buona parte" [Not all Italians did dance badly but "Buonaparte," or most of them, did]. Buonaparte was Napoleon's original Corsican name. The great general shone on the battlefield, but fumbled in the ballroom, it seems.

One of Freud's other examples concerned a young patient who was asked if he ever masturbated. The patient's answer was sure to be: "O na, nie!" [Oh, no, never!] But that "never" masked the whole story. Onanie or onanism is the common German word for masturbation.

Freud had many critics, but few were as sharp as G.K. Chesterton whose priest detective Father Brown has been popular since 1910. Chesterton provided a first-class punch line to his verses on Professor Freud.

The ignorant pronounce it Frood,
To cavil or applaud.
The well-informed pronounce it Froyd,
But I pronounce it Fraud.

Father Brown and the sense of evil

Like William James and Conan Doyle, the Catholic G.K. Chesterton was interested in religion. His dumpy priest detective often stressed that what he heard in the confessional helped him understand criminal behaviour.

Chesterton was a fine author and critic. He mocked, "the whole modern world has divided between those who make mistakes and want to fix them" and those who prefer not to. In *Heretics*, he wrote of Shaw:

> After belabouring a great many people for a great many years for being unprogressive, Mr. Shaw has discovered, with characteristic sense, that it is very doubtful whether any existing human being with two legs can be progressive at all.

Chesterton's autobiography claims he and Shaw played cowboys in a silent film that was never released. The British Film Institute is now trying to find it as it would be a wonderful curio.

The first Father Brown stories appeared in 1910. The priest has an acute sense of evil but is always ready to forgive as it is his duty to make sinners repent. One of the pleasures of the stories is his many tussles with the mastermind of crime, Flambeau. Poor Flambeau is always worsted and is sometimes on the verge of giving up his evil ways.

In his autobiography, Chesterton discussed "the genuine psychological reason for the popularity of detective stories," and demolished some clichés. "It is not true, for example, that the populace prefer bad literature to good, and accept detective stories because they are bad literature," he said. He had no intention of writing bad literature and, while the Father Brown stories sometimes read as if they had been written in a hurry, they are still worth reading. Many of the later stories were produced to make money, and Chesterton admitted in 1920 that "I think it only fair to confess that I have myself written some of the worst mystery stories in the world."

The Blue Cross was published in 1910 when a Eucharist Congress brings priests from all over the world to London. Valentin, the head of Paris detectives, has come to London hoping to catch the "colossus of crime" Flambeau, who is very tall and can be playful; he once made a judge stand on his head. In a similar vein, Flambeau ran the Tyrolean Dairy company "with no dairies, no cows, no carts, no milk but with some thousands of subscribers."

Valentin looks for Flambeau in unlikely places because the man is so elusive. Valentin does not think Flambeau is more intelligent but "the criminal is the creative artist; the detective only the critic." Except in the case of Father Brown perhaps.

Spiritual and philosophic truths matter more to Father Brown than scientific details. His work as a priest helps his work as a detective. He told Flambeau once: "Has it ever struck you that a man who does next to nothing but hear men's real sins is not likely to be unaware of human evil?" In *The Secret of Father Brown*, he revealed his empathy with criminals. He explained:

> You see, I had murdered them all myself. ... I had planned out each of the crimes very carefully. I had thought out exactly how a thing like that could be done, and in what style or state of mind a man could really do it. And when I was quite sure that I felt exactly like the murderer myself, of course I knew who he was.

The story of the *Blue Cross* develops into a splendid wild goose chase during which Valentin chances on some inexplicable things. In a café, salt has been put in the sugar bowl. In another restaurant, a seemingly respectable priest throws soup on the walls and then pays three times the amount of the bill. Then a grocer complains someone has changed the labels on his produce so that oranges and nuts are mixed up.

Valentin follows the two priests to a shop near Hampstead Heath where one of them had bought some peppermints and left a parcel. He asked the shopkeeper to mail the parcel to an address in Westminster. Valentin then sees the two priests discussing points of theology until the tall one, who is Flambeau, threatens the shabby cleric. If he does not hand over the parcel with the Blue Cross, he will "pull him to pieces like a straw doll."

Father Brown refuses to hand over and asks if Flambeau is sure the cross is in the parcel. When he was a curate in Hartlepool, three of his flock had spiked bracelets. Some criminals wore that to signal they belonged to a wrongdoing clan. One taught him the tricks of switching parcels which he just did without Flambeau noticing. Flambeau does not believe the little priest could do that. When he grabs the parcel, Father Brown points out they are surrounded by Valentin and a group of policemen.

The Blue Cross safe in Westminster, both Valentin and Flambeau bow to "the little master," while Father Brown shambles to find his umbrella. If Holmes was obsessed with the physical, Chesterton's Father Brown was obsessed with the metaphysical.

A Marxist view

Detectives attract unexpected fans. The Italian Marxist theorist Antonio Gramsci thought the Father Brown stories "delicious" and argued:

> Father Brown is a Catholic who pokes fun at the mechanical thought processes of the Protestants and the book is basically an apologia of the Roman Church as against the Anglican Church. Sherlock Holmes is the "Protestant" detective who finds the end of the criminal skein by starting from the outside, relying on science, on experimental method, on induction.

Father Brown, Gramsci continued,

> through the refined psychological experiences offered by confession and by the persistent activity of the fathers' moral casuistry, though not neglecting science and experimentation, but relying especially on deduction and introspection, totally

defeats Sherlock Holmes, makes him look like a pretentious little boy, shows up his narrowness and pettiness. Moreover, Chesterton is a great artist while Conan Doyle was a mediocre writer, even though he was knighted for literary merit; thus in Chesterton there is a stylistic gap between the content, the detective story plot, and the form, and therefore a subtle irony with regard to the subject being dealt with, which renders these stories so delicious.

Dorothy Sayers read Chesterton's essay on detective fiction and liked it which was not surprising because he included an academic flourish tracing the appeal of the detective story back to Homer, the kind of joining up of unexpected associations she liked as we shall see.

Is the detective story a modern *Iliad*?

Chesterton brought in Homer's epic when discussing the appeal of the detective story. "The first essential value of the detective story lies in this, that it is the earliest and only form of popular literature in which is expressed some sense of the poetry of modern life." When Chesterton was young, the Belgian poet Verhaeren made his name all over Europe with visions of the tentacles of the spreading city. Chesterton went on to suggest that "in its portrayal of a great city itself as something wild and obvious the detective story is certainly the 'Iliad.'"

Chesterton had an interesting view of the appeal of the detective story. He said, "the hero or the investigator crosses London with something of the loneliness and liberty of a prince in a tale of elf-land." He continued, "Anything which tends, even under the fantastic form of the minutiae of Sherlock Holmes, to assert this romance of detail in civilization, to emphasize this unfathomably human character in flints and tiles, is a good thing," because it allowed "the average man to look imaginatively at ten men in the street even if it is only on the chance that the eleventh might be a notorious thief." Ever inclined to the spiritual he added:

> men's souls have stranger adventures than their bodies, and that it would be harder and more exciting to hunt their virtues than to hunt their crimes. But since our great authors (with the admirable exception of Stevenson) decline to write of that thrilling mood and moment when the eyes of the great city, like

the eyes of a cat, begin to flame in the dark, we must give fair credit to the popular literature

which celebrates the common. The romantic possibilities of the modern city led to the popular detective stories, "as rough and refreshing as the ballads of Robin Hood."

Detective stories also worked as

by dealing with the unsleeping sentinels who guard the outposts of society, it tends to remind us that we live in an armed camp, making war with a chaotic world, and that the criminals, the children of chaos, are nothing but the traitors within our gates.

He added,

The romance of the police force is thus the whole romance of man. It is based on the fact that morality is the most dark and daring of conspiracies. It reminds us that the whole noiseless and unnoticeable police management by which we are ruled and protected is only a successful knight-errantry.

Chesterton loved putting seemingly opposite ideas and images together to make a startling, and usually funny, point. In his essay "Two Kinds of Paradox," he quipped that he often saw the word *cosmic* misprinted as *comic*, but that "the two are much the same."

A good example of such a paradox is at the end of *The Queer Feet* (1910), when Father Brown faces the wealthy and elite members of a dining club, ironically called "The Twelve True Fishermen," and returns stolen silverware that he has taken from the repentant crook. When the club members ask about the thief, the priest responds:

"I don't know his real name ... but I know something of his fighting weight, and a great deal about his spiritual difficulties. I formed the physical estimate when he was trying to throttle me, and the moral estimate when he repented."

"Oh, I say—repented!" cried young Chester, with a sort of crow of laughter.

Father Brown got to his feet, putting his hands behind him. "Odd, isn't it," he said, "that a thief and a vagabond should repent, when so many who are rich and secure remain hard and frivolous, and without fruit for God or man?"

Four years after the first Father Brown stories, the First World War started. Sayers tried to go to France to help in a hospital. Agatha Christie worked as a nurse's assistant which was hard, but also handy, as she picked up a knowledge of poisons – and of Belgian refugees. She used the former in her plots and the latter in her creation of Poirot. Before 1916 detective fiction had little interest in the psychology of the individual as Poirot liked to put it, giving his little grey cells an ego boost on the way. Christie's other great detective, Miss Marple, not being foreign, never boasted of her little grey cells, but she did not need to. The commissioner of Scotland Yard said she had the best detective mind in Britain. Christie's novels and Sayers' Lord Peter Wimsey would be influenced by the 1914 war, which changed so much.

Chapter 6

The First World War, mental illness and shell shock

The work of Rebecca West and the detective novels of the 1920s

In 1918, Grafton Eliot Smith and Tom Pear argued in *Shell Shock and Its Lessons* that the conditions of the war were unique. "Never in the history of mankind have the stresses and strains laid upon the body and mind been so great or so numerous as in the present war," they said.

But the strains of war had a long history. Deuteronomy 20:1–9 made clear military leaders knew many soldiers had to be removed from the frontline because of nervous breakdowns. The Greek historian Herodotus reported the first case of chronic mental symptoms caused by sudden fright in his account of the Battle of Marathon. Epizelus became blind "without blow of sword or dart" and never recovered his sight.

Twenty-four hundred years later Gilles de la Tourette, who first described Tourette's syndrome, published an article on hysteria in the German Army, which infuriated the German Chancellor Bismarck. In the Russo-Japanese War of 1904–5, the Russian Army set up a hospital to deal with psychological casualties, an innovation French and German medical journals discussed. But the 1914 war dwarfed all previous wars with more powerful weapons being used than ever before. It was a military and political watershed. Both of Freud's sons served in the military. Agatha Christie worked as a nursing assistant. The American Army used the then novel I.Q. tests to decide if recruits should be sent to fight. The founder of behaviourism John B. Watson was called in by the American Army. He was sent to France to work out how to persuade soldiers not to get involved with French women who were likely to give them venereal disease.

DOI: 10.4324/9780429344664-6

One little-known incident may have had far-reaching consequences. Hitler suffered from hysterical blindness in 1917 when he was a dispatch rider. Dr Edmund Forster at Pasewalk Hospital on the Belgium border had been influenced by Freud's ideas and cured the future Fuhrer who insisted on going back to carrying messages on the front lines. His cure convinced him he was destined to fulfil a special mission.

A medical speciality became a topic for public debate. Some 10% of British officers suffered from shell shock according to a 1915 article in *The Lancet* by Charles Myers. Many deserted, and hundreds were shot for cowardice.

Rebecca West's first novel, *The Return of the Soldier,* was a study of a shell-shocked soldier who was cured by psychoanalysis. Her lover H.G. Wells was a friend of W.H.H. Pitt Rivers, the psychiatrist who worked with Myers and was one of the most exotic scientists of the time. He co-founded the *British Journal of Psychology*, travelled the Pacific, studied then unknown tribes, was friendly with Ernest Jones and spent time with George Bernard Shaw.

The legacy of the war was brilliantly caught by Herbert Read who wrote a poem addressed to a conscript in 1940. He mourned that his body may have returned from the 1914 war but his soul did not. It had been destroyed.

Those who returned and yet were destroyed, dead or as we put it now burned out included Berkeley Cox, and Dorothy Sayers' third husband as well as Lord Peter Wimsey and Captain Hastings though he was less affected. Miss Marple lost the young man she loved. Poirot never served in the war as he was a senior man in the Belgian police. The war changed lives and fiction.

In his *History of the Psychoanalytic Movement,* published in the year the 1914 war started, Freud detailed the steps by which psychoanalysis attracted supporters. Until 1907 he was isolated but then "the situation changed at one stroke contrary to all expectations." Eugene Bleuler, one of the most famous psychiatrists of the time, told him psychoanalytic texts and ideas had been studied and made use of in Burgholzi, his hospital in Zurich. One of his colleagues came to visit Freud in Vienna. A year later the first psychoanalytic congress decided to set up the first psychoanalytic journal which was edited by Carl Jung.

In 1909, Freud was invited to America to give five lectures at Worcester College. During that visit, Freud met William James and James Putnam who had "expressed an unfavourable opinion of psychoanalysis but now he rapidly reconciled himself to it, and recommended it to his countrymen." Freud also praised A.A. Brill, the first man to translate his works into English, and Ernest Jones, who would become his official biographer. The two helped make psychoanalysis popular in the English-speaking world.

Six months after the war broke out, Freud wrote two essays in which he argued the war made it necessary for people to repress the horrors of deaths at the front. He was prescient because thousands of soldiers suffered "shell shock."

Wilfrid Owen's *Anthem for Doomed Youth* caught the terror of the front well.

What passing-bells for these who die as cattle?
– Only the monstrous anger of the guns.
Only the stuttering rifles' rapid rattle
Can patter out their hasty orisons.
No mockeries now for them; no prayers nor bells;
Nor any voice of mourning save the choirs, –
The shrill, demented choirs of wailing shells;
And bugles calling for them from sad shires.
What candles may be held to speed them all?
Not in the hands of boys, but in their eyes
Shall shine the holy glimmers of goodbyes.
The pallor of girls' brows shall be their pall;
Their flowers the tenderness of patient minds,
And each slow dusk a drawing-down of blinds.

Clement Attlee was a Major during the war and also wrote poetry about the trauma in the trenches.

The doctor who first described the effect of Owen's wailing shells was Charles Myers who kept a war diary, which he began when he returned to Paris in August 1914 after a climbing holiday in the Alps. The city was in turmoil. Long queues formed outside banks as people tried to withdraw money before it lost all value. When Myers got on the train for London, the restaurant car would only take payment in gold or silver.

In the winter of 1914, *The Times* medical correspondent found that many men who had not been under fire before wanted to know the feelings of those who had been. His conclusion was harsh: "The presence of such dwarfed and ill-developed creatures can be attributed only to the conditions of life created by our industrial development."

Fiona Reid in her *Broken Men* has dissected the differences in class between the officers and men. The officers, Reid found, were generally felt to be suffering from neurasthenia while working-class men were hysterical.

In August 1914 while Charles Myers was travelling in France, he met a businessman who "described the utter insufficiency of the surgical work at Dieppe." The man offered him his house if he would only set up a medical facility. Myers went on to Paris where most people were dressed in black and cattle were grazing near the Bois de Boulogne. He visited academic celebrities including Henri Bergson who remains famous for his work on 'elan vital', the life force.

After visiting Paris, Myers began to see soldiers who were returning from the front. He wrote, "the stories they told were often ghastly." One man had seen a German shoot a wounded British officer quite against the "rules" of war. Another man told him he had witnessed Germans overrun his trench and kill 16 wounded men, firing on some and bayonetting others.

It was only in December that Myers saw the first psychological cases as he came to describe them. His first patient was a 20-year-old private who had tried to disentangle himself from the barbed wire when a shell burst near him. At once his sight became blurred. Then another shell was "like a punch on the head with no pain after it." The explosion smashed his haversack, bruised the side of his body and burned his fingers. He lost his sight and his sense of taste and smell too. When acid was placed on his tongue, he reported no taste but "a peculiar feeling as if it dried the tongue."

Myers was still inclined to attribute the trauma to physical causes like a lesion in the brain. The more patients he saw, however, the more he had doubts. He saw hundreds of shell-shocked patients. Three case histories will suffice. He listed a 25-year-old corporal who was buried for 18 hours after a shell blew up the trench in which he lay. A second case was that of a 23-year-old private who had been "blown off a heap of bricks 15 feet high due to a shell bursting close to him." Both men had been unconscious and had lost their senses of taste and smell. The corporal could not identify a strong solution of salt (reporting only that "it feels like petrol does on the hand") and failed to smell peppermint, ether, iodine tincture or carbolic acid. With his left nostril, the second patient failed to detect the smell of peppermint, ether, iodine tincture, eucalyptus or ammonia, but he recognised all but iodine with the right nostril. Both men also suffered from amnesia.

Myers had studied with Pitt Rivers, and the latter is a central figure in shell shock. His first books *Delirium and Its Allied Conditions* (1889), *Hysteria* (1891) and *Neurasthenia* (1893) dealt with subjects Freud also studied. Then Pitt Rivers travelled to Jena to study experimental psychology, and while there he started a diary where he noted: "I have during the last three weeks come to the conclusion that I should go in for insanity when I return to England and work as much as possible at psychology."

After travelling twice to the Pacific, Pitt Rivers returned to England in spring 1915 and worked at the Maghull Military Hospital near Liverpool. The hospital had been influenced by Freud. It used techniques such as dream interpretation, psycho-analysis and hypnosis to treat shell shock.

After about a year Pitt Rivers was transferred to Craiglockhart War Hospital near Edinburgh. There, again, he treated officers who had been diagnosed with "shell shock." Pitt Rivers did not see them as failures. He argued that brave men could succumb to overwhelming fear and, remarkably, that the best cure was neither patriotism nor hatred of the enemy. It was the love of soldiers for one another.

Like Jung, Pitt Rivers thought Freud exaggerated the power of sex. He saw the instinct of self-preservation rather than the sexual instinct, as the driving force behind war neuroses. For all that he believed in what he called catharsis and Freud called cathexis. Bringing repressed memories into consciousness robbed them of their power. Know thyself and it won't be so bad, to put it crudely. Pitt Rivers spent most of his days talking with the officers at Craiglockhart. He concentrated on, first educating the patient about the basics of psychology and second making the fear seem normal. Soldiers learned their symptoms were not "strange" nor permanent. War experiences were traumatic so to try to repress all memories of them was not "mad." Once a patient could under-stand the sources of his troubles (which could be conscious, un-conscious, environmental or a combination), he was on the way to being cured.

Pitt Rivers dissected "danger instincts," into five: (i) fear as mani-fested by flight, (ii) aggression as manifested by fighting, (iii) the suppression of all emotion in order to complete complex tasks to make one safe, (iv) terror as manifested by immobility which was what much of life in the trenches was like and (v) collapsing to escape from the fear. Typically, when all five "self-preservation" instincts are repeatedly aroused for long periods of time, such as during exposure to war, the instincts gain power and eventually "escape" from the unconscious.

Pitt Rivers proposed that officers and soldiers who suffered from night terrors did so because they were trying to repress emotions back into the unconscious. Repression, however, as both Freud and Pitt Rivers knew, does not banish conflict; it just keeps it bottled up in the unconscious. As a result, repressed emotions along with their associated emotions and memories seep into consciousness when soldiers are sleeping, and they suffer from night terrors.

Pitt Rivers encouraged his patients to express their emotions in a time when society encouraged men to keep a "stiff upper-lip." His method, and his deep concern for every individual he treated, made him famous among his clients including the writers Robert Graves, who wrote *I Claudius*, and Siegfried Sassoon.

Sassoon wrote in a letter to Robert Graves (24 July 1918)

O Rivers please take me. And make me
Go back to the war til it break me ...

Pitt Rivers did not wish to "break" his patients, as he knew that it was their duty to return to the front and his duty to send them there. He published the results of his experimental treatment of patients at Craiglockhart in *The Lancet*, "On the Repression of War Experience," and recorded interesting cases in *Conflict and Dream*, which was published a year after his death.

Shell-shocked patients were neither malingering nor physically injured, Myers decided. Their symptoms were "functional," the result of strictly psychological trauma. His patients resembled those that in civilian clinics would have been labelled "hysteric."

Andre Leri, a French doctor, recorded in detail the power of the weapons. Some left atrocious physical injuries, but Leri also wrote of "emotional" patients in ways very similar to Myers. He generalised "with haggard eye, pinch nose, pale face and bewildered air he will throw himself down in the most distant corner of the (nursing) station, on the ground ..., hiding himself there, shrinking and will not move again." These patients trembled, breathed with difficulty and "seemed not to understand anything." If they were faced with fragments of a shell they would cry out "No, major, I will not go in there, shells are falling now."

The army was confused by the dilemma of mental illness. Wounded soldiers were meant to be heroes injured by enemy action, but shell-shocked men had many symptoms that mentally ill patients had. The way these two groups were paid reflected stigma. Wounded men were entitled to special pensions, while the mentally ill were not.

Society still had its class distinctions too. A letter in *The Times* also displayed the stiff upper-middle-class lip with brio. A public school man trying to find his way to his headquarters met an Irishman, who "regaled" him with his account of life in the trenches:

> It was a piece of luck because when I started out I was quite sure I was going to be in a devil of a funk and when it was all over I was mighty surprised with myself to find I had been too much interested and amused by the Irishman to take in there were bullets buzzing about.

He concluded that the rattling rifle fire made less noise than "a public school field day."

Perhaps Winston Churchill provides the best example of the cavalier public school attitude in the trenches. After the failure of Gallipoli, he had to resign from the Cabinet and volunteered for the front. He crossed the Channel to re-join his old regiment, the Oxfordshire Hussars as a relatively humble major but was soon promoted to lieutenant colonel.

One of his officers, Andrew Gibb, wrote *With Winston Churchill at the Front*. Gibb quoted Churchill saying, "war is a game to be played with a smiling face," and Churchill certainly got a laugh when he addressed his first parade. "War has been declared," he said, paused dramatically, and added, "on lice." Gibb claims that it was in Churchill's unit that the term deloused was invented.

The Great War lasted nearly five years, and public attitudes to the wounded changed twice. There was some sympathy at first for the shell shocked but, as one casualty wrote on arriving at Netley, the main military hospital, "we were not the battle-stained heroes who were expected." There was confusion between the normally sane soldiers who had simply been unable to cope and "real" lunatics. Two years into the war, however, the public became weary of the subject and less sympathetic.

The threads of time shimmy in odd ways through one's writing. In the mid-1980s a psychiatrist friend, the late Dr James MacKeith, asked me to meet his father. Stephen MacKeith had been an important figure in British psychiatry. He served for five years as a senior psychiatrist in the army from 1940 on. I got to know him well because his son asked me to help him finish a book on imaginary worlds that some children create. When Stephen brought me the manuscript, I could see why he had been unable to get it published; it was nearly 1000 pages long. I agreed to help.

While we worked together Stephen explained to me that almost all psychiatrists of his generation were proud that no deserters from the British Army were executed during the Second World War. In the First World War 346 had been, even though it was obvious some men simply could not cope with the stress of battle.

The novels

Perhaps the first novel to deal with shell shock was written by H.G. Wells' lover, Rebecca West. She was just 24 when she published *The Return of the Soldier*. The book explores what we now call post-traumatic stress disorder, and with a touch of adultery. Chris Baldry returns from the trenches having lost his memory so that he does not even remember that Kitty is his wife. He is attracted to an earlier lover who has married another man, but she is still a little in love with Chris. The confusions of love and sex do not deter the upper class from playing tennis. As it becomes clear that Chris needs help from a psychoanalyst called Gilbert Anderson who performs one of the fastest analyses ever. He informs Chris that he is the patient "with the detective tone" and then manages to deal in record time with his patient's problems. Analysis interminable it is not.

Chris is not heroic which has led one critic to say West challenged the existing notions of "stable masculinity." That seems an over-intellectual way of putting it; a touch of the Freuds and his subconscious scrubbed clean, Chris recognises his wife and stops longing for his earlier lover. The book ends before we discover whether they live happily ever after. It is unlikely as Kitty resents the fact that her husband forgot who she was for a while at least. Amnesia? Shamnesia more like.

Freud's ever-loyal ally, Ernest Jones, also wrote a paper on war shock which led to

> an extensive release of previously tabooed tendencies, a release shown in endless ways, for instance, even in the language of camps, and on the other hand the acquiring of a strict discipline and self-control along lines widely different from those of peace times.

Jones gave as an example a young woman who had never been able to marry

> the sexual sides of her-nature with her ego ideal, and whose only way of dealing with that aspect of life has been to keep it at as great a distance from her consciousness as possible. If now she gets married it may happen that she will find it impossible to effect the necessary reconciliation.

Obliged to become sexual she will develop neurotic symptoms. Jones added:

> The moral attitude towards fear, and the conflicts arising in connexion with it, remain the same in war as in peace. In both cases it is considered a moral weakness to display or be influenced by fear, and especially to give in to it at the cost of not doing one's duty.

The army agreed with that continuing its policy of executing deserters.

Jones was sharp. "The soldier who would like to escape from shell fire is, so far as moral values are concerned, in the same position as a man in peace time who will not venture his life to save a drowning child."

The detective novels of the 1920s often faced up to shell shock and its legacy. Hastings in Christie's *The Mysterious Affair at Styles* has gone to rest in the countryside to recover from the trenches. Wimsey never forgets that Bunter saved him and soothed him through episodes of depression. It is striking that very few became crazed psychopaths, however. Nevertheless, the detective authors could not escape the shadows of the war. Conan Doyle lost no fewer than 11 family members either in combat or to disease, his eldest son and only brother among them, and as a result some of the above factors might have met with a fierce, if not overwrought, need to prove his dictum, "There is no death."

By the time the Christmas 1920 edition of *The Strand* appeared with the front-page banner headline "Fairies Photographed: An Epoch-Making Event Described by A. Conan Doyle" roughly half the world – including the likes of Harry Houdini – was convinced he was disturbed. Conan Doyle's faith in the occult persisted though. When Agatha Christie disappeared for 11 days after her first husband left her in 1926 Conan Doyle became involved in trying to find her and called in a medium. The other side failed to reveal her whereabouts. The *Daily Mail* headlined "A Sub-Conscious Plot" but could not decide if she had really lost her mind, lost her memory or was just rehearsing a new plot. Christie eventually turned up in a hotel in Harrogate and said nothing in her autobiography about why she disappeared. Christie dissected the motives for murder but always remained guarded about her innermost self.

Chapter 7

Freud, psychoanalysis and the psychology of Agatha Christie

The golden age of detective fiction

In 23 cases, the murderer in Christie's books was a doctor, a statistic that reflected her family's bad experiences with the profession. Her father was a rich stockbroker and her mother was the daughter of an army captain. Christie was educated at home and spent two years at a finishing school in Paris. She was used to dealing with doctors as social equals (or even inferiors, as they had to use the tradesman's entrance). They would be invited to dinner only as a favour, so she felt no need to be obsequious towards them. Her mother was a frustrated would-be doctor who read the *British Medical Journal* and the *Lancet*, and considered herself as being as fully trained as her son Ernest who had to abandon medicine because he had a phobia which crippled his career; he could not stand the sight of blood.

When Christie's father became ill, he was diagnosed by different specialists, first as having kidney disease, then a heart condition and finally a gastric problem. No surprise then she sniped that medical science was "of little use." When her mother was ill after a trip from Paris, the doctors again could not make up their minds. She might have appendicitis, or gallstones, or paratyphoid or something else.

Christie had been a nurse, but her experience of hospital left a lot to be desired: "one never learned what a 0.1% solution meant, yet such substandard individuals tended to be venerated as higher beings just because they worked in hospitals."

Seeing doctors as dangerous Christie would not have been surprised to learn Freud himself had blood on his hands. He had committed one murder and almost killed a second patient. Ernest Jones, his loyal biographer, avoided any honest description of why

DOI: 10.4324/9780429344664-7

Emma Eckstein or Fleischl Maxlow died. What drove Freud in both cases was his faith in, and addiction to, cocaine.

In 1895, Emma Eckstein came to see Freud with depression and problems related to her menstrual cycle. He diagnosed hysteria and "masturbating to excess." He called in Wilhelm Fliess, an eccentric nose and throat specialist who was for years Freud's closest confidant. Fliess looned that operating on the nose cured every sexual problem. He and Freud cauterised Eckstein's nose with cocaine. After the operation, they bandaged her up and sent her home.

Two weeks later, she returned to Freud with unstoppable nose-bleeds.

Freud had the sense to call in a different doctor to inspect her nose. It saved Eckstein's life. The second doctor pulled out 20 inches of gauze that Freud and Fliess had left inside her. As the second doctor removed the gauze, blood poured uncontrollably from her nose; her eyes bulged, and she turned white.

Over the next few days, Eckstein returned to Freud with near-fatal haemorrhages. Half of her face had caved in. Freud continued treating her, giving her morphine and reapplying bandages, but he felt enormous guilt over what was a very basic surgical mistake. Eckstein recovered slowly, forgave Freud – and astonishingly became an analyst herself.

A recent case history had made Freud interested in cocaine. In 1884, he read an article about a German soldier who had collapsed from exhaustion, and, after swallowing cocaine, stood up and walked "easily and cheerfully with a pack on his back." Looking for his big break in medicine, Freud ordered a gram of pure, unadulterated cocaine – and swallowed a twentieth of it. He found it gave him energy "without any of the unpleasant after-effects that follow exhilaration brought about by alcohol." Cocaine was magical. "One senses an increase of self-control and feels more vigorous and more capable of work." He enthused, "One is simply normal, and soon finds it difficult to believe that one is under the influence of any drug at all."

Oblivious to cocaine's addictive properties, Freud prescribed it to his friend and teacher, Ernst von Fleischl-Maxlow, who was a morphine addict. Freud thought cocaine could cure him, but it did not. Fleischl-Maxlow went from being a morphine addict to being a cocaine addict and, within months, died of cocaine poisoning.

As the evidence against cocaine became irrefutable, and his fame grew, Freud quit coke and destroyed the letters and documents that showed he had used it. In *Freud on Coke*, I suggested Freud may not have needed the drug anymore, as he had made his reputation following *The Interpretation of Dreams*. "I know very well how [the cocaine episode] happened to me," he wrote to his friend and biographer, Fritz Wittels, in an attempt to remove all mention of his cocaine use. "The study on coca was an allotrion [a distracting, futile pursuit] which I was eager to conclude."

By the end of the war, Freud was a major figure if still controversial. In the early 1920s, Hollywood offered him the then huge sum of $5,000 for the right to film his biography. He turned it down, and there is still only one proper biopic. John Houston commissioned a script by Sartre which had to be rewritten because it was so long. The eventual film with Montgomery Clift is intense and excellent. One of the intriguing examples of Freud's influence in the 1920s can be found in Noel Coward's play *The Vortex*. The mother commits adultery; her son is furious. A production still of the original production shows Coward who played the son with his arms around his mother's legs. The play could have been called Oedipus in the West End.

Christie would not have been surprised Freud used cocaine and was to all intents and purposes a killer, though unlike most of the doctors in her books, his motives were not wholly evil. A paper in the *British Medical Journal* in December 2010 compiled the number of killer doctors in Christie's books. She started with her first as in *The Mysterious Affair at Styles*, a doctor tries to cover up a murder. In her first play, *Black Coffee*, a doctor is the prime suspect. In her last book, *The Postern of Fate*, a doctor is one of the two murderers.

Killer doctors – all of them men – appear in the following among others.

In *Cards on the Table*, Dr Roberts murders his lover's wife, and also a rich man in whom she confides, by putting anthrax on his shaving brush. Roberts's other victims include witnesses to his crimes. He comments that he has "always been interested in crime. Bad thing for a doctor, perhaps mustn't say so to my nervous patients!"

Dr James Alfred Kennedy, a GP and psychiatrist, is the triple killer in *The Sleeping Murder*. He is in love with his half-sister Helen, and when it becomes clear she might marry someone else he strangles her. He then pretends Helen has eloped, forges letters supposedly from her which show she was a nymphomaniac and gives her father drugs that lead to his detention in an asylum.

Miss Marple catches the doctor as the killer in the 4.50 from Paddington. He had to kill his wife because she was a Catholic and would not divorce him leaving him free to marry a rich woman. Dr Quimper in *Murder She Said* is another greedy doctor who plots to marry an heiress after doing away with the remaining members of her family, including his own estranged wife. In *Four-and-Twenty Blackbirds*, Dr Lorrimer tries to inherit the family fortune by murdering a rival claimant.

In one short story, Dr Rose tries to hypnotise a nun and then subjects her to the kind of word association test Carl Jung developed. Some of the nun's associations are odd. What could link destruction with sea? Christie then finishes with the notes Dr Rose made on his patient. His last one runs: "Am I mad, or should I be Superman with the power of death in my hand?"

Sometimes the doctor gets what he long deserved. In *Elephants Can Remember*, the victim is Professor Willoughby who spent years inflicting hydrotherapy and electroshock therapy at the institute he founded. He is drowned in the bath he used for the therapy.

John Lanchester in a penetrating essay has argued that Christie was fascinated by form; the books discussed in this chapter illustrate that and pose devilish puzzles. Christie loved doing that, but her puzzles also show her interest in psychology.

Detectives are often annoying and implausible, but nobody is more so than Poirot, as Christie herself acknowledged. "Would anyone go and 'consult' him?" she wondered aloud. "One feels not." He was, she said, "regarded perhaps with more affection by outsiders than by his own creator." She warned writers to be starting out on a career in detective fiction: "Be very careful what central character you create – you may have him with you for a very long time!" Miss Marple was more sympathetic. Christie described her as "an elderly, gossipy lady in a small village, who pokes her nose into all that does or does not concern her, and draws deductions based on years of experience of human nature," yet Marple is fundamentally believable in a way Poirot is not.

The A.B.C. Murders, an apparently pathological puzzle

Poirot gets a letter signed "A.B.C.," that details a crime that is to be committed very soon. Two similar letters soon arrive, each before a murder is committed by A.B.C. Alice Ascher, in her to-bacco shop in Andover is the first victim; then "Betty" Barnard, a flirty waitress, is killed on the beach at Bexhill; third, the rich Sir Carmichael Clarke is killed in Churston. An ABC Railway Guide is left beside each victim.

Poirot wonders why the letters were sent to him, rather than to the police or the newspapers. He is also puzzled when the third letter arrives late as his address has been misspelled. Soon A.B.C. sends his next letter, which foretells that a man whose name starts with D will be murdered in Doncaster, the day when the St Leger will be run. A man in a cinema is stabbed but his name does not start with D.

The police then get a tip-off about a man linked to the murders – Alexander Bonaparte Cust, an epileptic travelling salesman, who has memory blackouts and constant agonising headaches. He sustained a head injury during the 1914 war and has shell shock. Cust illustrates many themes currently in psychiatry then. He flees and returns to his room in acute anxiety. He goes to the Andover police station, where he is taken into custody. He claims that a stocking firm hired him and told him to go to all the towns where there was a murder, but he cannot remember committing any of them.

Poirot doubts Cust's guilt because of the man's memory black-outs, and his extreme anxiety. The killings are so calculated that Poirot feels Cust cannot be guilty. As ever Poirot is right. Carmichael was killed by his brother who wanted to make sure he would inherit his estate.

Christie's next book is also a triumph of form and psychology.

The doctor narrator

In The Murder of Roger Ackroyd, Christie set herself a devilish puzzle. The narrator is a village GP. The idea for what is perhaps Christie's most famous thriller came partly from her brother-in-law who said that what he would like "is a Watson who turned out to be the criminal." At much the same time Lord Louis Mountbatten suggested to Christie that it would be interesting if the narrator of a book turned out to be the murderer. She first thought about the technical problems that would cause and then, her mind "boggled" at the thought that Hastings might turn out to be a killer. She soon decided Hastings did not have violence in him. But the challenge of that puzzle inspired her, and she defended herself against the charge that she had cheated by omitting key details from her narrator's account. She insisted that she gave readers all the clues needed to arrive at the solution.

The victim is a wealthy 50-year-old, Roger Ackroyd, who is engaged to Mrs Ferrars whose husband died a year before the book starts. Then she is found dead herself having committed suicide. Her doctor James Shephard is a friend of Ackroyd's who asks him to discuss the tragedy urgently. Shephard is a little vain and fancies himself as an expert on psychology and the unconscious.

After seeing Ackroyd and going home, Shephard gets a call telling him Ackroyd has died. He rushes to the house to find the butler denies having made any such call. Shephard insists they make sure Ackroyd is alive. When he does not reply, they force the door open to find him stabbed; the weapon is an exotic Tunisian dagger. The time of death is crucial; two witnesses heard Ackroyd speak at 9.30 p.m., a time every possible suspect has a solid alibi.

Poirot has recently moved into the nearby village to retire; it is strange that such a cosmopolitan man should bury himself in the English countryside, saying he has done so as to engage in his preposterous hobby of growing gigantic marrows. When Flora Ackroyd, the niece of the victim, discovers Poirot's identity, she asks him to investigate because she is worried her fiancé will be suspected.

The narrator shows much arrogance, a trait of many serial killers. Dr Shephard lets Poirot see the shed where he tinkers with clocks and other gadgets, a fatal error as it reveals he has mechanical skills. At one point Poirot comments that a man may change under pressure and he believes that has happened in this case. Shephard treated Mrs. Ferrars and her husband. When the husband died, Shephard realised his wife had poisoned him and started to blackmail her. He then lost most of the blackmail money in foolish investments.

Finally, Poirot confronts Shephard in private and offers him the chance to commit suicide. On the last night of his life, Shephard writes that he had hoped to publish his account as one of Poirot's failures. In his apologia at the end of the book, he says he did encourage Ackroyd to read the letter which proved the doctor knew Mrs. Ferrars had killed her husband and that he had been blackmailing her. "Or let me be honest – didn't I subconsciously realise that with a pig headed chap like him it was my best chance of getting him not to read it." Shephard also comments that Ackroyd's nervousness was "interesting psychologically."

Shephard is proud that he did not actually lie in his text. For example, he told readers that when he found Ackroyd dead that, "I did what little had to be done." One of those small tasks involved removing a Dictaphone Ackroyd had bought. To confuse the question of when the murder was committed, Shephard triggered the Dictaphone to play at a time when his sister could vouch for the fact that he was at home. He removed Dictaphone by stuffing it into his doctor's bag and taking it away.

The book has an interesting subplot. It was published in 1926 before any of the Marple books. Christie wrote that when the idea of turning *The Murder of Roger Ackroyd* into a play was mooted, she was told it needed a love interest. Christie minded the idea of replacing Shephard's elder sister with a younger woman to provide that. She liked the character of the sister Caroline who seemed to know everything that was going on in their village. "I liked the idea of village life reflected through the doctor and his masterful sister … I think at that moment Miss Marple was born."

In his recent book on Miss Marple, the literary critic Peter Keating argues that snobbish critics have ignored Christie's references to Freud and his ideas. His *Agatha Christie and Shrewd Miss Marple* only deals with Marple who, spinster though she is, understands the power of sexual attraction, a subject Christie often discussed in her autobiography. She wrote of the flirtations of the 1920s and conveyed her fascination with sex. Keating argues many murders in Christie's books revolve around lust, pushing men and women to the edge, making them indifferent to the suffering of any innocent people caught up in their schemes.

Christie got it wrong

Earlier I pointed out that Pierre Bayard had revised *The Hound of the Baskervilles*. Bayard has also suggested that Christie got it wrong with *The Murder of Roger Ackroyd*. Bayard provides an intertextual frisson whose pattern is clear:

Freud influences Christie,

Christie uses Freud's ideas.

But did her own unconscious lead her to making the wrong character the killer?

Bayard has the brio to suggest Agatha Christie and Conan Doyle decided on the wrong killer in three of their books and this is possible as the writer is not wholly the writer or perhaps really the writer at all. Bayard's analysis called *Who Killed Roger Ackroyd* has actually some sharp points as he suggests it is not the doctor who is the killer. He fixes on Dr Sheppard's sister as guilty. Her motive is to protect her brother which is perhaps plausible. Bayard stresses the point the narrator makes in the book that Caroline knew everything that went on in the village. So she must have known her brother blackmailed Mrs. Ferrars. Bayard adds: "The psychoanalytic disassociation of the character leads us to place the character of Caroline in opposition to the character of Poirot. It leads us to reformulate our initial question asking this time, who killed Dr Shephard?"

Bayard, however, ignores the fact that Christie said Caroline inspired Miss Marple.

Bayard makes much of the aggression that Poirot displays to Hastings as "an obscure almost sado masochistic hatred in displayed." Poirot is sometimes rude to Hastings, and sometimes teases him about women; true, but there is no example of him being cruel to him.

The critic John Lanchester argues that *The Murder of Roger Ackroyd* is the great modernist novel and then suggests formalist might be a better word. "Christie's techniques were in many respects devoutly unexperimental but her books are a systematic exploration of formal devices and narrative structures, all through a genre with strictly defined rules," Lanchester states. She loved the game of playing the genre. Lanchester states, "it's quite difficult to think of an idea she didn't try, short of setting a Poirot novel in a school for wizards." He also admits he has had the odd experience as a reader in that that you often forget, "until you're a significant way in, that you've read the book before; and even after that, you quite often forget whodunnit." Lanchester adds that *Ordeal by Innocence* is another instance in which the psychological atmosphere is distinctly oppressive. Unlike Sayers' Wimsey, who sometimes is tormented by doubt when he knows the killer he has caught will hang, neither Poirot nor Marple ever regrets catching a killer. Evil needs to be punished.

Lanchester argues that *Murder on the Orient Express* is also a formal masterpiece.

Murder on the Orient Express

In Istanbul Poirot overhears a conversation between a very proper British colonel and an efficient English woman Mary who says to him, "Not now ... when it is all over." We learn nothing else.

Christie had travelled a number of times on the Orient Express, once when the train had been delayed for 24 hours after a landslide. Two years earlier it had been caught in a snowdrift and stuck for six days. These delays became key to her plot.

At dinner, an American millionaire approaches Poirot. Rachett wants protection from his many enemies. Poirot refuses the commission. Then during the night Rachett is stabbed twelve times. Poirot's friend Bouc, an officer of the Wagon Lit company, begs him to investigate. In the dead man's compartment, Poirot finds a series of clues Holmes would have relished – a pipe cleaner, matches and a scrap of burnt paper. Poirot demands a hat box, puts the scrap under the metal frame which holds the hat and lights a match. Briefly some writing appears, and Poirot sees the name "Daisy." That is enough to tell him Rachett was actually a Mafia hood called Cassetti who was responsible for kidnapping Daisy when she was three years old and the child was killed.

I have said that I started to read Christie to understand Englishness, but the Orient Express only has three proper English passengers – the colonel, the woman he loves and Ratchett's valet (brilliantly played by Gielgud in one of the many films of the book). The valet likes reading romantic novels.

Christie could be playful about her writing self. Under the name of Mary Westmacott, she wrote romantic fiction though never a book called Love's Captive *which Rachett's valet is reading. Mrs. Oliver who writes detective novels herself also appears in a number of her books, and sometimes you feel Christie is making fun of herself. Poirot is amused by the fact that Mrs Oliver is often struggling with what to do next with her sleuth Sven. So we have a writer of detective stories creating a writer of detective stories as a character.*

On the Orient Express Christie allows herself to play with stereotypes. The Italians are loud, the Germans are efficient, the French suave, the Hungarians ridiculously formal. The Russian princess a fantasy from Tsarist days.

Poirot remains confused by the crime and the welter of clues. He suspects the British colonel, but as with Cust, the psychology is wrong. The colonel might well murder, but he would never stab someone twelve times in a disorganised frenzy. One must respect the psychology of the crime Poirot insists; Bouc also insists on that, but his ideas are laughable. He suspects the Italian car salesman, but only because Italians never need an excuse to stab; they are addicted to the stiletto.

Gradually Poirot senses that this was not an impromptu crime, but coolly planned and well organised. The colonel gives Poirot a clue whose importance he does not realise at once, when he says that trial by a jury of twelve good men and true – and of course it was men at the time – is a sound system. Apart from Poirot there are twelve people on the carriage, and the murderer could only be one of them.

Poirot works out that each of the twelve passengers had a connection to the Armstrong family. The aged Russian princess Dragomirov is the godmother of Countess Andreyani, who is the younger sister of Daisy's mother. Foscarelli, the Italian "stabber," was the family chauffeur. The wagon lit conductor is the father of Armstrong's housemaid who was suspected of helping the kidnapper and killed herself in despair. Finally the pattern falls into place so Poirot can explain how he arrived at the solution.

Poirot tells the passengers: "I saw it as a perfect mosaic, each person playing his or her allotted part." At the start of his explanation Poirot says there are two possibilities. The simple one is that the murder was committed by some Mafia enemy of Rachett's who sneaked on to the train. His second theory is that all the twelve people on train were involved. Rachett deserved to die. The twelve formed the jury the colonel had mentioned. Poirot leaves it to Dr Bouc to decide which is the correct explanation. Bouc decides it was a Mafia revenge hit and reverts to his prejudices. The Italians are known for their vendettas as well as their stabbings.

The book has been much filmed. A 1974 version starred Albert Finney who over-acted very unusually for him. Recently Kenneth Branagh and John Malkevitch have played Poirot. In *Poirot and Me*, David Suchet, who played Poirot in the TV series, said that the detective was in torment for much of the time and accounted for that in a way which highlights Christie's concern for justice. Poirot wrestled. Suchet wrote, both his Catholic faith and his moral reasoning once he arrived at the solution. His faith tells him murder is evil. "He wants to please God and stay true to his belief that part of his role in life is to defeat evil," Suchet wrote, but Poirot also knows – and the comparison with Father Brown is striking – that sometimes people deserve to be forgiven. Suchet adds he was sure that when Poirot went back to his compartment he did not just pray "for God's guidance" but was also painfully aware he might not be able to follow it. Suchet made sure that when Poirot walked away from the train he was holding his rosary. Poirot also prays God to forgive him for lying but then God is just, and justice has been done by those whose friends and family suffered so much.

The madness of psychiatrists

In the 1970s I was told that somewhere in the United Kingdom there was a secret psychiatric clinic whose only patients were psychiatrists who had gone mad. I failed to find this clinic but even the rumour of its existence indicated a great cultural shift. In the last 50 years there has been an interesting variation on the theme of the dangers of madness as the evil psychiatrist has become a common character in fiction.

Psychiatrists have even more power than other doctors since they can have patients detained. In Christie's day lobotomy was common. Asylums were cruel. Mary Jane Ward's 1946 novel, *The Snake Pit*, presents a disturbing account of a patient's experience in a huge state mental hospital, where ECT, lengthy confinement and freezing baths are treatments. (A teenager in Broadmoor in the late 1970s made identical complaints in a film I made.) In *The Snake Pit* a nurse realises: "They were going to electrocute her, not operate upon her ... What had you done? You wouldn't have killed anyone and what other crime is there which exacts so severe a penalty?"

Psychiatrists were also perverse. *Electricity*, by Victoria Glendinning, has a shocking account by a fictional psychiatrist, who glories in his assault on a mute, five-year-old girl. She is a perfect victim because she cannot tell anyone of the horrifying experience Dr Bullingdon inflicts on her.

Those little mad girls, all slack-bodied and soft, great eyes, perfect skin. Examining them ... you can imagine. Sometimes they scream. There was this little one with long dark hair, bright eyes, she would not speak, never made a sound, never let anyone touch her, so they brought her to me. She let me touch her. But she was rigid. She knew I wanted to rip her open to fuck her warm little guts.

Bullingdon then casually notes: "She died. Children die so damned easily."

However, fiction exaggerates the criminality of psychiatrists it seems. Rather few cases where psychiatrists have committed murder have come to light. The most sensational was that of Dr Bouwer. He had to leave South Africa shortly after the South African Health Professions Council declared him an "impaired doctor" because he was addicted to pethidine. This did not prevent him from becoming the head of psychological medicine at Dunedin Hospital in New Zealand. Once there Bouwer drugged his wife and was found guilty of murder. Lust and money were his motives. He had fallen in love with Dr. Anne Walshe who believed he was innocent, stating, "He did not murder his wife and he is not a cold, calculating murderer. He's a very gentle man."

Bouwer's sister-in-law claimed he had told her New Zealand was an ideal place to commit the perfect murder. Bouwer had also told students that injecting someone between the toes with insulin was the perfect way to commit a murder. Arrogance again!

And Then There Were None – every motive under the sun

Bayard also offered his "truer" version of And Then There Were None. Christie said that once she had the idea for the book, seeing it through convincingly was a challenge, which again she loved.

The story is a variant on the locked room mystery, but the locked room is an island. Soldier Island is a mile off the coast of Devon. Eight people have received a tempting invitation to go there. Thomas and Ethel Rogers, the butler and cook-housekeeper say their hosts, Mr. Ulick Norman Owen and his wife Mrs. Una Nancy Owen, have been delayed.

A framed copy of a nursery rhyme, Ten Little Niggers (called "Ten Little Indians" or "Ten Little Soldiers" in later editions), hangs in every guest's room, and there are ten figurines on the dining room table.

The drama begins the first night after supper. A voice (which turns out to be a gramophone record) accuses each visitor of having committed a murder, and escaped justice. It then asks if any of "the accused" wishes to offer a defence. The first in the dock or in the coffin as it turns out is Anthony Marston, a dashing and callous young buck ran over two people because he was speeding, but his only punishment was to be banned from driving for a year. After dinner, Marston tosses down a whisky and immediately dies. Christie's inevitable doctor Dr Armstrong confirms that there is no cyanide in the drink. So how did he die?

One of the macabre pleasures of the book is a nice touch of form. Christie makes each murder fit a verse in the rhyme. Marston chokes to death just as the verse foretold:

Ten little soldier boys went out to dine
One choked his little self and then there were nine.

The butler's wife faints and is taken to her room. The next morning, she too is found dead. Some of the guests suspect her husband of poisoning her to stop her confessing to the murder of an old woman they were looking after. The second verse has also come true:

Nine little soldier boys sat up very late
One overslept himself and then there were eight.

Dr Armstrong knows that 15 years earlier he killed a patient when he was too drunk to operate but he managed to hush that up. Another guest, General MacArthur, was accused of killing one of his junior officers who was having an affair with his wife. By lunchtime, General MacArthur has been killed as his head was smashed in.

Dinner is still served, of course. But the guests begin to suspect that U N Owen is systematically murdering them. They work out that U N Owen is really unknown; they are at the mercy of an unknown killer.

The group also includes Philip Lombard, a man with a shady past and a retired judge. Justice Wargrave says not one of them can be ruled out as the murderer. Another guest, Blore, turns out to be a corrupt Scotland Yard detective. The voice accused Blore of having committed perjury to get a man convicted. The man died in jail. Blore was not found out but promoted for the conviction.

On the second morning, the boat that usually comes to the island every day does not arrive. Then the butler Rogers is found dead while chopping wood which fits another verse.

Seven little soldier boys chopping up sticks;
One chopped himself in halves and then there were six.

After breakfast, Emily Brent, who dismissed her maid simply because the girl was pregnant, is found dead in the kitchen. She has been injected with potassium cyanide.

The voice accused Justice Wargrave of influencing the jury to hand a guilty verdict to Edward Seton, a man, many thought, was innocent of killing an old woman. The unjust judge deserves death.

The last woman still alive Vera Claythorne was accused of letting a boy in her care drown because she was obsessed with Hugo, a young man who would inherit a fortune if the boy died. When Vera goes upstairs to take a bath, she is shocked by the touch and smell of seaweed and screams; the remaining guests rush upstairs to her room. Wargrave, however, is still downstairs. When the others come back, they find him dead – with a judge's wig on his head. Dr. Armstrong examines him and states what seems obvious; the judge was shot in the forehead. Again this fits the verses; five little soldier boys going for law:

One got in Chancery and then there were four.

In the morning, they signal SOS to the mainland but get no reply. Blore returns to the house to eat, only to be killed by a heavy statue that crushes his skull. Since neither of them was near the house when the death occurred, Vera and Lombard conclude that Armstrong is the killer.

Christie develops well the growing paranoia in the house as each of the survivors suspects the others. There are many references to psychology as she describes their feelings of helplessness.

It is soon clear, however, that Dr Armstrong cannot be the killer as Vera and Lombard find his body washed up on the beach. The last two alive each conclude the other must be guilty. Vera suggests moving the doctor's body away from the shoreline as a gesture of respect for the dead, but this is a pretext. While moving the body, she steals the gun Lombard has had on him. When he lunges at her to get it back, she shoots him dead.

Shaken, half in a dream, Vera returns to the house. She finds a noose and chair arranged in her room, and a strong smell of the sea. She knows she let the boy in her care drown, is wracked with guilt and hangs herself, which fits the last verse of the rhyme.

One little soldier boy left all alone

He went and hanged himself and then there were none.

Scotland Yard detectives finally reach the island. They try to reconstruct the deaths with the help of the victims' diaries.

The book ends with a postscript found in a bottle caught inside some trawling nets. The postscript is a confession by the judge. Christie was concerned to make the unbelievable believable and gives Justice Wargrave a shrewd psychological assessment of himself.

As a child, he discovered he liked killing insects, a typical psychopathic trait so he went into the law. As a judge, he protected the jury from "the emotional effect of emotional appeals by some of our more emotional counsel."

Wargrave prides himself on the fact that he never allowed an innocent person to be found guilty, but he also discovered he had "a savage bloodlust." For most of his life, he satisfied both desires as a judge who had no inhibitions about sentencing murderers to hang. That satisfaction became too abstract as he got older and then was diagnosed with a terminal illness.

To achieve the murders he had to fake his own death. Given her tendency to make doctors the murderer, Christie makes Dr Armstrong the willing accessory. When Wargrave seemed to have been shot, the doctor examined him. No one else got a close look at the body, however. No one challenged Dr Armstrong. In fact, there was just a round red stain mark on his head, but only Armstrong knew it was not blood. The others believed Wargrave was fatally injured.

Wargrave's confession adds, "It may be understood – I think a psychologist would understand – that my make up being what it I adopted the law as a profession." That worked for years but finally he decided to devise "for my own amusement the most ingenious way of carrying out a murder." He did not kill at random; his victims were themselves murderers but could not be prosecuted under the law. Although he wished to create an unsolvable mystery, he acknowledges in his confession a "pitiful human need" for recognition.

Many critics stressed the puzzle element. For *The New York Times Book Review* (25 February 1940), Isaac Anderson said,

> When you read what happens after that you will not believe it, but you will keep on reading, and as one incredible event is followed by another even more incredible you will still keep on reading. The whole thing is utterly impossible and utterly fascinating. It is the most baffling mystery that Agatha Christie has ever written, and if any other writer has ever surpassed it for sheer puzzlement the name escapes our memory. We are referring, of course, to mysteries that have logical explanations, as this one has. It is a tall story, to be sure, but it could have happened.

Maurice Richardson in *The Observer* issue of 5 November 1939 was impressed saying that:

Ten Little Niggers is one of the very best, most genuinely bewildering Christies yet written. We will also have to refrain from reviewing it thoroughly, as it is so full of shocks that even the mildest revelation would spoil some surprise from somebody.

Christie wrote that "austerity and the tight discipline that goes to making a tight detective plot is good for one's thought processes." According to Pierre Bayard, however, her thought processes were again all too imperfect. There is a French saying *de l'audace avant toute chose*, daring before anything else, and it applies to Bayard's analysis of the book. He asks a number of questions including how do we know that Wargrave wrote the confession? It could have been forged. Bayard is not convinced by many details. He points out that it is very unlikely the apparently dead Wargrave could have been carried back to his room without showing any sign of life. This is a nice point. Bayard also does not believe that even as a judge Wargrave could have known of so many instances of killers going unpunished. A policeman would be better placed to do that – Blore was a policeman.

Bayard also supplies a motive which, to be fair, Christie hints at. As he had been corrupt, Blore needs to bury his old identity. Bayard argues that unconsciously Christie used a similar device to that of *The A.B.C. Murders*. The important murder is hidden among a number of murders. Apparently, dead Blore is free to start on a new life. It is an ingenious revision.

The Teacup Poisoner and *Curtains*

Just before her death, *The Daily Mail* accused Christie of giving the English serial killer Graham Young his murderous ideas. Young, who was nicknamed the Teacup Poisoner, had studied poisons and chemistry from an early age. *The Daily Mail* claimed he had got the idea from Christie's (1961) novel *The Pale Horse*, and that she had inspired him to murder three and poison seven others. The truth was very different. One of the psychiatrists at Broadmoor, the late Edgar Udwin, was very poor at assessing how dangerous his patients still were. He recommended the release of eight men who went on to kill again. Graham Young was one of those who took advantage of Udwin's professional naivete.

Loyal to her readers Christie wrote the last case for Poirot which took place, like his first, at Styles. She called the book *Curtains*.

Styles, once a grand family house, now a rather seedy hotel. Poirot is old, wheelchair-bound, dying but still avid for justice. "The brain is as magnificent as ever," he reassures Hastings who is as adept as ever at looking on with exasperated admiration.

A finale often demands a touch of sentiment. Hastings by now has a daughter who is in danger of her falling for a Fascist cad who believes that those who lead useless lives should be eliminated. For Poirot, any murder is a sin. He examines his own life and feels he has perhaps been too self-righteous, too conscious of rectitude. He writes to Hastings: "It is my life's work to save the innocent – to prevent murder and this is the only way I can do it." The truly guilty man, who has killed a number of victims whose lives he felt did not benefit society, "could not be touched by the law." Poirot could think of no other way the killer could be defeated than by killing him.

Miss Marple, whom Christie identified, was never killed off.

Chapter 8

Individual psychology and the inferiority complex

Lord Peter Wimsey and the work of Dorothy Sayers

The characters authors sometimes create reflect their own character – and their own fantasies. The supreme example of this is Lord Peter Wimsey, the man who was everything the men in Dorothy Sayers' life failed to be. She could be acerbic about her hero, however, and once noted that he emerged from "his top hat like a maggot emerging from a gorgonzola."

Oddly for a whodunnit Sayers' most famous book *Gaudy Night* does not have one murder, but it is rife with violence and observations on psychology and especially on the inferiority complex which led to a break between Freud and Alfred Adler who created analytic psychology. In a way that would have been too intellectual for Christie, Sayers refers to ideas about the inferiority complex throughout a book many consider her masterpiece *Gaudy Night*.

More than any of the authors discussed, Sayers' life affected her fiction. As a child she was precocious. She devised and acted in plays which were staged in her parents' house, a rectory as her father was a vicar. She was very excited when she discovered things were not isolated but joined up, and that when they were joined up, they formed patterns. Her parents often took her to the theatre which became an enduring love. "I dramatized myself and have at all periods of my life continued to dramatize myself" making herself the heroine, but she adds that she always realised "I was the creator, not the subject of these fantasies." When she was thirteen she was enthralled with Dumas' *The Three Musketeers* and staged a version where her father played Louis XIII. By then she had started to write poetry which she continued to do all her life.

Sayers went to a boarding school at the age of twelve and sailed through the exams to be admitted to one of the new colleges for

DOI: 10.4324/9780429344664-8

women in Oxford. In 1912 in her first year at Somerville, she met Roy Ridley who won the Newdigate Prize for poetry; she fell madly in love with him on the spot. His name was "like the hero of a six penny novelette," she wrote. Ridley then went down from Oxford "so I shall see him no more. My loves are always unsatisfactory as you know," she told a friend. She turned her unsatisfactory love into a paragon, and Ridley became the model for Wimsey. Both men went to Balliol.

Oxford was affected by the 1914 war. Belgian refugees came to the city, and some were bemused by its habits. Sayers wrote of an aristocratic Belgian lady who refused to associate with the head of the committee for Belgian relief because she had seen Miss Bruce ride a bicycle.

Sayers continued with poetry and submitted poems to Basil Blackwell, who accepted them for his series *Oxford Poetry*. Moved by accounts of what soldiers were suffering in the trenches, she tried to go to France to work for the Red Cross, but she was too young to be accepted. She also tried to join the Board of Trade but failed in that too. To make a living she had to take a teaching job, but in 1920 she gave it up to move to London. She had no prospects, but she was brimming with ideas and reading works of criminology in the Reading Room of the British Museum.

Enter Wimsey on stage

On 22 January 1921, Sayers wrote to her mother that she was

> visited with ideas for a detective novel and a Grand Guignol play. My detective story begins brightly with a fat lady found dead in her bath with nothing on but her pince nez. Now why did she wear a pince nez in her bath?

The reader who could work that out could work out who the murderer was, Sayers told her mother.

Sayers was also toying with writing a story in the manner of a Sexton Blake story but that turned into something different, the first Wimsey book. In "How I came to invent the character of Lord Peter," written in 1936, Sayers said she did not remember inventing Wimsey at all. He walked into her detective story "complete with spats" – and also with a complicated family pedigree. It is reasonable to argue she did not remember inventing him because he answered a pressing emotional need. After all, writers express, and also repress, their obsessions.

Sayers gave Wimsey a detailed background and even a psycho-sexual history. He first appeared in the draft of a play called *The Mousehole*; the stage directions describe him as sleek, fair, dressed in a perfect grey suit except when he wears a luxurious dressing gown – a matinee idol or a preux gentleman as Wodehouse's Bertie Wooster often called himself. Sayers admired Wodehouse. Her play was never staged and possibly never finished.

So Wimsey made his debut in *Whose Body*, the most gruesome of Sayers' novels, and many aspects reflect the horrors of the war that had just finished. She could never have contemplated a hero without intellectual distinction, so after Eton, she dispatched Wimsey to Balliol College where he got a first in modern history. His uncle then sent him to Paris where, as British aristocrats often did, he sowed his wild oats. Wimsey's entry in Who's Who, as Sayers wrote it, listed as his hobby other people's business, perfect for a detective.

The war changed Wimsey's life. He was a Major in the rifle brigade and a conscientious and effective commanding officer, popular with his men; he retained their affection as it becomes evident in *Gaudy Night*.

In the army, Wimsey met Sergeant Mervyn Bunter who figures in most of his stories. Unlike the ineffectual Hastings and Watson, Bunter is almost an equal partner. In 1918, Wimsey was wounded by artillery fire and buried alive. The trauma caused a breakdown, and he was eventually sent home. Wimsey was for a time unable to give servants any orders since his wartime experience made him associate the giving of an order with causing the death of the person to whom the order was given. With typical understatement, Wimsey's mother, the Dowager Duchess referred to her son being in "a jam."

Wimsey and Bunter agreed that if they survived the war, Bunter would become Wimsey's valet. Bunter usually addresses Wimsey as "My Lord" but he is a friend as well as a servant, and Wimsey often praises Bunter's competence. He can gain people's confidence, is an excellent photographer and is knowledgeable about poisons.

With the approval of the Dowager Duchess, Bunter moves Wimsey to 110A Piccadilly, one of the best addresses in London. For years, however, Wimsey would relapse into depression; then

Bunter would take care of him. "He braces me with a continuous cold shower of criticism."

Harriet Vane, Sayers' heroine, does not feature in *Whose Body* but first appears in *Strong Poison*. She writes detective novels which suggest Sayers identified with her. When Wimsey sits in the public gallery watching Harriett's trial, he decides she is the one woman for him. Their first encounter is dramatic. Harriett has been accused of the murder of her lover, Philip Boyes whom she refused to marry. She is in the cells waiting for the verdict when Wimsey goes to see her. Despite a judge's summing up against her, the jury cannot arrive at a verdict and so she will be tried again. Wimsey thinks she is not guilty and promises to use the time before her retrial to prove her innocence.

Wish fulfilment is part of the title of this chapter for a reason. What Sayers craved and never quite got was the love of a good man who was her equal. She found it possible to be frank about some wish fulfilments, but they were less essential than finding her perfect love. She was hard up when the war ended, so she made Wimsey rich as "it gave me pleasure to spend a fortune for him." When she was dissatisfied with living in a cheap lodging – a single room – she put him in a luxury flat. When her cheap rug had a hole in it, "I ordered him an Aubusson carpet." When she had no money for a bus fare, she conjured up a Daimler for him. "I can heartily recommend this inexpensive way of furnishing to all who are discontented with their incomes." Imagining a perfect carpet was easy to admit; imagining a perfect love less so – and Sayers never suggested Wimsey made up for all her imperfect lovers. Only her first, and worst, was an intellectual as she made Wimsey. She also gave Wimsey many of her own characteristics. He is clever and loves logical disputation. He is an avid reader too as well as the author of *The Murderer's Vade-Mecum* as well as of a book on incunabula, or books printed before 1501.

Wimsey has a social conscience. Sometimes he is ashamed of the pleasure he takes in detection. He reads *The Physiological Bases of Conscience* because his conscience troubles him especially when his detection ends with a killer being hanged. Wimsey quotes a passage in the book:

> you could carve passions in the brain with a knife, you could get rid of imagination with drugs and cure an outworn convention like a disease. The knowledge of good and evil is

an observed phenomenon attendant upon a certain condition of the brain cells.

(The British Library catalogue has no record of such a book incidentally.)

The description of how Wimsey arrives at solutions echoes the Gestaltists theory. Sayers wrote:

> He remembered – not one thing but another thing, nor a logical succession of things. but everything, perfect, complete in all its dimensions as it was and instantaneously.

In her first novel, *Whose Body*, the dead man has Semitic features, and the police assume him to be a Jewish financier, Reuben Levy. Wimsey knows at once "with the evidence of his own eyes" that the man cannot be Jewish as he is not circumcised. The corpse also has bad teeth and hands which are too rough for a rich man.

Sayers sent the novel to a literary agent Andrew Dakers who loved it. The publishers he found asked her to cut out any reference to circumcision and she agreed.

When she started the book, Sayers did not foresee how her own troubled love life would be reflected in the relationship between Wimsey and Harriet Vane. In 1921, the year when she began to write *Whose Body*, Sayers met John Cournos, a modernist poet and a Jew who had been born in Kiev.

As both she and Cournos were writers, each left versions of their relationship. Cournos gave the most detailed. In one scene of his novel *The Devil Is an English Gentleman*, Stella – who is the Sayers character – invites him to dinner. After they have eaten they lie down on a couch piled with cushions. He undresses her and then takes off his own clothes. They caress each other "with languid passion, deliberately restrained as if in fear of the consequences of excess. She did not resist him, and he might have taken her." Cournos harps on the contradictions. "Though she desired to be taken she inwardly held out against him and refrained from speaking the magic word he wanted to hear." Cournos believes she is thinking that if she lets him take her, he will forsake her. He imagines she thinks, "I must have him forever or not at all."

Cournos waits for "the generous gesture, for a token of abandonment on her part; it did not come." His not-quite lover wants him to marry her, but he wants her to give herself to him there and then. He leaves her flat at 1 a.m. and spends the night in a hotel. A week later, the scene repeats itself. After some more torrid meetings, she is still holding out. "I'm not sure I can stand the restrictions of free love," Stella says – which was true of Sayers to some extent at least.

Cournos answers he is not sure he can stand the restrictions of married love. In reality, Sayers offered to marry him according to English law, which would leave him free to divorce her in America if he got tired of her. She told him in a letter that she had a "careless rage for life and secrecy tends to make me bad tempered ... precautionary measures cramp the style. Bah if you had chosen I would have given you three sons by this time."

When Cournos left her Sayers became depressed. She accused him of every dirty trick invented by civilisation to avoid the natural result. "There is always the taint of the rubber shop now." The rubber shop sold contraceptives, of course.

Cournos wrote that "grief had put a stamp on her features." For her part, she complained he had a depressing effect on her. She once tramped all over London to find a film he would "condescend to see" – and she had a bad blister at the time.

After Cournos left her Sayers met William White who was no intellectual but obsessed with motorcycling. She became pregnant by him and was determined to hide the fact from her parents. Concealing her pregnancy was not easy as had by now been hired by an advertising agency S.H. Benson. The job gave her financial security and the chance to do something she loved – playing with words. She became a very successful copywriter. A placard for the Toucan she devised to promote Guinness still hangs above a café in Soho. She did not want and could not afford to give up her job when she was pregnant, so she arranged for her friend Ivy to look after the baby. The decision forced her into secrecy which she claimed to hate, but she did not acknowledge the child was hers until he was nine years old.

In August 1924, Sayers wrote to Cournos, "I went over the rocks. As you know I was going there rapidly but I preferred it shouldn't be with you but with somebody I didn't really care two pence for. I couldn't have stood a catastrophe with you." If she sought help for going over the rocks, she left no record of it.

There was some author-like comradeship though. In January 1925, Cournos sent her the article on detective fiction Chesterton had written. She thanked him and replied that Chesterton had identified the central difficulty that of making the solution neither too obvious nor too obscure; it had to be "something previously known, and it ought to be prominently displayed."

The relationship between Wimsey and Vane was far more decorous than Sayers' never-quite consummated affair with Cournos. When they first meet Wimsey asks her if she and Boyes were friends. They were not, Harriet replies. Boyes wanted devotion. She gave him that, but he also needed to test her, just as Cournot had tested Sayers. Harriet says she hated "being on probation. I quite thought he was honest when he said he didn't believe in marriage – and then it turned out to be a test." Wimsey snipes that it seems the man was a prig. The affair made her feel ridiculous, Harriet concludes. Wimsey is glad Harriett feels slighted by Boyes.

Then Sayers springs a surprise on the reader but perhaps less of a surprise on those who know her history with Cournos. Wimsey says that when this is all over, he hopes Harriet will marry him. This is the stuff of romantic novels, love at first sight, love when the hero saves the damsel in distress. Sayers, however, invests Harriet with a coolness she never had with Cournos. Harriet is flattered but unmoved. Wimsey is not one of those, she snipes. She has had 47 proposals of marriage already. Is he the 48th? If you are notorious men want you.

Harriett also assumes Wimsey will be put off by the fact that she has had a lover. Wimsey replies he has had many himself and could even produce testimonials of competence in bed. "I'm not trying to blackmail you into matrimony," he adds saying he would investigate the case anyway. Harriet does not want a proposal made out of pity though. Wimsey still walks away from her "light-headed," as she has made clear she does like him.

Strong Poison centres on the investigation rather the romance, and Wimsey finds out who the killer really is – a cousin of Boyes. Greed made him kill; he had tried to destroy a will that would have made Boyes, who was always struggling financially, a rich man. In a number of subsequent books, the game of love and resistance between Harriet and Wimsey goes on. By refusing him Harriett, who seems weaker, is in fact stronger.

After *Strong Poison* was published and her son was born, Sayers met a Scottish journalist, Max Fleming. Again the wounds of the war lasted long, Fleming had been gassed and some of his brothers had been killed, and a third badly injured. At least Mac, as he called himself, was straightforward, and for years the marriage was happy. Slowly, however, the legacy of shell shock caused problems. In 1930, she wrote to a friend that Mac was now "so queer and unreliable it is not safe to trust him to do anything at all." He was prone to more and more fits of temper.

Real life, real fiction

That same year Sayers with Robert Eustace published *The Documents in the Case* (1930). Wimsey played no part. The book was very much based on a real case, that of Edith Thompson.

When she was 15, Edith met Percy Thompson who was three years older than she was. Eleven years into what seemed to be happy marriage, the couple met Frederick Bywaters who was just 18. Edith was immediately attracted to him, and they became lovers.

When Percy found out he confronted the pair. Bywaters demanded that Percy divorce Edith; Percy ordered him out of their house. Edith later told the police that after Bywaters left, Percy hit her several times and threw her across the room. His alleged violence did not stop her meeting Bywaters again.

Despite his violence, the couple went to the theatre together. On 3 October 1922, Edith and Percy went to the Criterion Theatre in Piccadilly and caught the 11.30 p.m. train back to Ilford. As they walked home from the station, a man jumped out from some bushes and attacked Percy. Edith was knocked to the ground; the attacker fled. By the time police arrived Percy was dead, and Edith was distraught. When a police sergeant took her back to her house, she said to him, "they will blame me for this." At the police station the following day, officers told her that Bywaters had confessed to the murder. Edith then gave details of their affair.

The police then discovered more than 60 love letters she had written to Bywaters. They made clear she wanted nothing more than the death of a now-superfluous husband, who also had the knack of not dying. Edith had fed him mashed potatoes with ground glass and after that failed with arsenic. Percy did not even get sick. Given a husband who refused to die, Edith now begged her lover to "do something desperate."

One of the detectives who investigated the murder later wrote, Edith's letters "played a great part in hanging her." Edith had the gift of words. She vividly described her unhappy marriage, her struggles at work or her delight in a fresh spring day.

Sir Henry Curtis-Bennett KC, Edith's barrister, urged her not to give evidence as the prosecution could only prove that she had been present at the murder. She ignored his advice. In his closing speech, Sir Henry pleaded that her immorality had to be seen as the "glamorous aura" of a "great love. He was lyrical:

> This is not an ordinary charge of murder ... . Am I right or wrong in saying that this woman is one of the most extra-ordinary personalities that you or I have ever met? ... Have you ever read ... more beautiful language of love? Such things have been very seldom put by pen upon paper. This is the woman you have to deal with, not some ordinary woman.

The jury was not swayed and found both lovers guilty. Edith became hysterical and started screaming in court, while Bywaters protested: "I say the verdict of the jury is wrong. Edith Thompson is not guilty."

Almost one million people signed a petition against their death sentences. Bywaters was admired for his fierce loyalty, and Edith attracted sympathy because hanging a woman was abhorrent. On the day of her execution 9 January 1923 in Holloway Prison, Edith collapsed in terror and became unconscious.

In one of the many discussions that followed, the barrister and author Edgar Lustgarten said Edith "was a remarkable and complex personality" and that the court was unable to understand questions of "sex and psychology" and the "consequent possibility of fantasy."

Psychology 1928

Sayers was familiar with the latest developments in psychoanalysis and also with the way psychology was changing advertising. John B. Watson had left academia and was working for J. Walter Thompson. He had been forced to resign his chair at Johns Hopkins because of a divorce scandal. Watson's contribution to advertising is clear from his own analysis of the campaign he devised for Johnson and Johnson. Their talcum powder had to shine with purity, and a baby had to be sprinkled with purity as soon as she or he was born – and powder used many times a day. Baby would feel good; mother would feel good.

I must again introduce a personal note. In 1974, I interviewed B.F. Skinner, the famous behaviourist. In 1928, he was at the start of his career and had abandoned his ambition to be a poet. Skinner did write two novels though neither involved murder since they depicted a utopian society where psychology creates good human beings. Skinner encouraged me to write a biography of Watson. As we shall see later, behaviourism led detective authors to focus on the minutiae of the behaviour of criminals. That took over 20 years though.

As Skinner started his psychological career, Sayers wrote her masterpiece.

Gaudy Night

The second chapter of *Gaudy Night* starts with a quote from Burton's 17th-century *The Anatomy of Melancholy*. Burton says that those who are troubled by melancholy are so "in company, out of company, at meat, at exercise at all times and places" and most of all they cannot forget it. But writing may be a solace.

The relationship between Wimsey and Harriet comes to a head in *Gaudy Night*. The inspiration for the book is easy to pin down. In June 1934, Sayers went to a gaudy at Somerville. The word comes from the Latin *gaudium* for "joy." Gaudies are an opportunity to celebrate with other members of the college, both from the same years of study and of different generations.

At one point Harriet is asked: "Is the writing of good prose an emotional experience?" She replies that if you get it right "there's no excitement like it. It makes you feel like God on the 7th day – for a bit anyhow." That was true of Sayers for some of the time.

The plot of the book is complicated. The question of women's education and of the need to defend the truth that obsesses some scholars make Gaudy Night a rich book. Three elements are relevant. First Sayers peppers the novel with references to psychological theory especially to theories of the inferiority complex which many well-educated women are said to suffer. At one point one of the dons, Miss Hillyard, comments of the students and teachers: "Though you will never say it everyone in this place has an inferiority complex. Never mind the intellectual achievements you all believe in our hearts we ought to abase ourselves before any woman who has fulfilled her animal functions." Childless women are lacking and know they are lacking.

Harriett herself frets she does not write as good books as she might. Sometimes there are mistakes in her plots but luckily readers do not seem to spot that. Also because of her sense that she is inferior to Wimsey, Harriett feels she has to rebuff his advances. Here her knowledge of psychology is no help. The fact that she knows all about her sense of inferiority does not help her get rid of it.

One of the students says of another, "Cattermole must have a man of her own. Does not matter who he is. It's her inferiority complex again."

The college exudes frustration. In one of Harriett's conversations with a don, a student is described as having "repressed emotional instincts." "The warped and repressed mind is apt enough to turn upon itself and wound itself," the don comments. "I believe," says Harriett, that "when you get the primmest people under an anaesthetic they are liable to bring the strangest vocabulary out of their subconscious – in fact the primmer the coarser." Repression will out.

The main plot centres on the fact that the college is plagued by a series of nasty notes and obscene drawings sent to various dons. The head of the college makes discreet enquiries and discovers hers is the only women's college to suffer from such obscenities.

As Harriett writes detective fiction, has been tried herself for murder and also has helped Wimsey solve one case, the college asks her to find out who is responsible for the notes. As women's education is controversial the college wants to keep the scandal secret and so will not call in the police. Harriett agrees partly because she wants to prove she can solve a case without Wimsey's help.

The book has many descriptions of Wimsey. At one point Harriet describes him as "nervy." One of the other gaudy guests dismisses that. The man has everything, so he deserves no pity.

Harriet then goes to Ascot where she becomes aware of "a pair of slim shoulders tailored to a swooning point and carrying a well known parrot profile." (It makes one recall the toucan.) But she is pleased not to be affected by seeing him. When Wimsey rings her later, she wants to decline his invitation to dinner but finds that she cannot. Wimsey is in acute pain as they eat, but hides it till Harriett drops her napkin and he struggles to do what a gentleman should do – pick it up. Wimsey says he is sorry to present himself in "such a decrepit state," and adds he knows he is doing that to get her sympathy. Later a friend tells Harriet Wimsey knows what he wants, while Harriett does not because she is too conflicted by her sense of inferiority.

Harriett's conflict about Wimsey is at the heart of the book. Once she even dreams he is embracing her. "This really will never do. My subconscious has the most treacherous imagination." She invokes Freud to help her dismiss the meaning of the dream. "If I really wanted to be passionately embraced by Peter I should dream of something like dentists or gardening." She wonders what truly murky feelings can "only be expressed by the polite symbol of Peter's embraces." But she can't help wondering what Peter would do with a case like this.

How could one, Harriet muses, understand other people's motives when one's own remains mysterious. The trigger for that thought is 1st April. She knows Wimsey will propose marriage again on that date by letter because he always does so on that day. Yet "why did one feel irritated about that letter and still fret when it did not arrive on time. There was no urgency about it since she knew what it would say, knew she would refuse but 'it was annoying to sit about expecting it." Wimsey likens his proposal to a repeated line in a farce.

After a girl nearly drowns, Harriett is threatened when she gets a note saying Your Turn Is Coming.

Wimsey then turns up unexpectedly at Balliol having completed his European mission. This section of the book is a turning point because he exposes his weaknesses to Harriet in a way he has never done before. They decide to go punting and their drift down the river makes Harriet realise: "It is there that it has happened, but it had happened long ago, the only new thing that has happened is that I have admitted it to myself."

The climax of the book is delayed when Wimsey recognises the college porter as a man who served under him in the trenches. "We thought you was gone that time," the porter adds. "When we saw yer at the bottom of that Boche dug out with a big beam across you."

"I had a bit of luck then," Wimsey says. That is not the end of the memories. The writers were never far from forgetting the trauma and how it affected the men of their generation.

Harriet has always resisted gifts Wimsey offers her, but now she let him give her a splendid set of the ivory chessmen. The chessmen are then smashed to bits. Wimsey is worried for her safety and persuades her to wear a dog collar to protect her if the culprit tries to strangle her. He is prescient as Harriett is attacked but saved by the dog collar.

Wimsey then takes away the dossier that Harriet has compiled on the events and teases her; she should know who is guilty given everything she has found out. He then disappears and when he returns he knows who the culprit is. The speculations about frustration have missed the point, he tells a gathering of dons.

One of the dons, Miss De Vine, once demolished a thesis written by a man called Arthur Robinson. Robinson never got his M.A. because she exposed some deceit in his work. Wimsey traced Robinson's history. Disgraced, Robinson took a job as a teacher at a school where they did not mind why he had been deprived of his M.A. He could not cope with the shame; however, he took to drink and was sacked. Then he killed himself.

Wimsey has also discovered that Robinson married and had three daughters. His wife Annie was devastated by his exposure, changed her name and went into domestic service. When she discovered that Miss de Vine had got a job at the college, she applied for a job there and became a scout. The word scout comes from ecouter or listening, but by the early 20th century, it referred to a servant who made the beds for undergraduates.

Once she was established in the college, Annie started to place the obscene messages. She hoped de Vine would be found responsible and dismissed.

Having tried and failed to kill Harriett, Annie hides in the college coal cellar. She is brought before the dons and de Vine denies all knowledge of Robinson's death. Annie replies: "You wouldn't have cared. You killed him. I say you murdered him," Annie says. De Vine flung "his children and me out to starve." Robinson's only crime had been to tell a lie about someone "who lived centuries earlier."

De Vine says it was her job to uphold scholarly standards of truth which makes Annie furious. "What business had you with a job like that. A woman's job is to look after a husband and children. I wish I had killed you. I wish I had killed all of you." Their ambitions for equality cause damage. Annie accuses them of taking work away from men.

After Annie is taken away, Harriet and Wimsey forgive each other.

Who was superior?

Inferiority is a theme of Gaudy Night, and it was also an issue among psychoanalysts from early on.

Freud was the first born and golden boy of his family. He was excellent at school and was given a room of his own, much to the annoyance of his sisters. He wrote that his mother's love gave him the confidence to be a conquistador. The contrast with Alfred Adler was dramatic. Adler was the second-born child and unhealthy. He found competition with his older healthy brother and rejection by his mother difficult. He felt eclipsed by his brother and resented "his favoured status in the family" (Hoffman, 1994, p. 11). To make matters worse, Adler was at the bottom of the class, Jewish – and stupid, could it get worse? But he buckled down and became a good student. He was compensating, a term he used in his theory.

Adler argued all infants have a feeling of inferiority as soon as they begin to experience the world. They need to gain their parents' attention which they do not always manage. Maimed, the child needs to make up by developing other strengths. With good nurturing and care, he/she can accept challenges, and learns they can be overcome with hard work. Thus, the child develops normally and develops the courage to be imperfect.

But many children do not get what is really practical love – and need to compensate, a process that goes awry. If feelings of inferiority become too intense, the child begins to feel as though he/she has no control over his/her surroundings.

The result is overcompensation. Adler (1917) used the ancient Greek figure Demosthenes, who had a terrible stutter but ended up becoming the "greatest orator in Greece." The Greek practised with marbles in his mouth which helped overcome the stutter – and ended up being a great orator. Winston Churchill also feared a speech impediment would hamper his performances when speaking – and sought help for that. Even King George VI, whose father was always teasing him for stuttering, managed to overcome this disability with the help of an eccentric therapist. So we can turn problems into strengths.

Sayers does not say much about Harriett's childhood, and so the reader knows little about why she feels inferior beyond the problems of being female in the 1920s. Wimsey is different. His mother does criticise him, but she loves him. He is intelligent, a gift of his genes. His supportive uncle makes sure he sows his wild oats in Paris. And the fact that he is aristocratic is hardly a cause for low self-esteem. Wimsey also manages to avoid being insufferably superior.

Adler (2013a) provided an example of a child with a superiority complex, who is "impertinent, arrogant and pugnacious" (p. 82). All because the little brat feels inferior.

According to Boeree (2006):

> Adler must be credited as the first theorist to include not only a child's mother and father and other adults as early influence on the child, but the child's brothers and sisters as well. His consideration of the effects of siblings and the order in which they were born is probably what Adler is best-known for. (p. 84)

Freud and Adler fell out, however, which was common among the analysts. Melanie Klein and Anna Freud hated each other, and Freud's translator, James Strachey, spoke of the "battle of the ladies."

The continuing drama

Sayers told Cournos she had a rage to live, and Wimsey tells Harriet something similar, "I know that the worst sin is to be joyless."

Harriet is touched and replies: "If I owe you nothing else I owe you my self respect."

Finally, at the end, Harriet gives in to her feelings. Wimsey says he will never ask her again to marry him and adds: "I can only say that if you will marry me it will give me great happiness." She puts her hands on his gown, but it is he who has to find the words, the words the man Sayers loved never said to her. The finale is in Latin, a language Sayers first tackled when he was six.

> "Placetne magistra."
> Does it please you, mistress?
> Placet, she replies, it does please.

In the end, they marry which does not stop them investigating more cases. Sayers gave her alter ego a happier marriage than she ever had.

I have stressed the appeal of puzzles and Sayers introduced puzzles into some of her fiction. In *The Fascinating Problem of Uncle Meleager's Will,* the will depends on solving a very long crossword puzzle which Sayers publishes in full in the story.

Sayers also placed her *Murder Must Advertise* in an advertising agency and would have been aware of both British and American campaigns and how psychology changed them. She wrote also in 1937 a paper on *The Psychology of Advertising*. In it, Sayers draws a parallel between the motives of advertisers used and the motives for murder. I quote her article at length because it shows the swagger of her style as well as her sharp psychological insight. Eighty years on, her manifesto explaining why advertising can be powerful still reads very well.

Sayers first discussed the disciplines of writing copy. She wrote:

> The task of the advertisement writer is excessively difficult; he has to persuade people to spend money on things they do not know they want.

Inertia (technically known as sales-resistance) is strongly en-trenched in the citadel of the soul, and it would be idle to expect the advertiser – faced by this colossal task – to be idealistic or over-scrupulous in his methods of attack. Like any other strategist, he assaults the weak places. Fear-gate, Sloth-gate, Greed-gate and Snob-gate are the four cardinal points at which the city of Mansoul can most effectively be besieged.'

In advertising, fear is less intense than of being exposed as a suspect in a murder but it still real. Sayers continues:

> By Fear-gate go in his formidable Death's-Head Hussars: Are you Suffering from Halitosis, Body-Odour, Athlete's Foot, Pains in the Back, Incomplete Elimination? Are you Insured against Sickness, Old Age, Unemployment, Battle?

Sayers then adds the question: "Are you afraid of Murder and Sudden Death? No ad sells a cream to stop that. She returns to questions of hygiene poking fun; "Is your Lavatory Clean? Does Dry-Rot Lurk in your Roof?" And there is always the fear that comes with love.

"Wave your Hair, under Pain of Losing your Husband's Love! Use Blank's Pure Dusting-Powder, under Pain of Poisoning your Baby! Beware of Substitutes! Beware of Germs! Beware of Everything!

By Sloth-gate go in the armies of Leisure; the Ready-Cooked Foods, the Chromium that Needs no Cleaning, the Clothes that

Wash Themselves, all the Gadgets and Machines that Take the Irk out of Work."

Greed made people kill and also made people buy. She added: "Greed-gate is the entrance for all the schemes that promise Something for Nothing. The magistrates of the city work very hard to close Greed-gate; Lotteries can now scarcely find entrance in this country; Free-Gift Coupons have received a shrewd knock and Guessing-Competitions and Pools have sustained severe reverses. But surprise parties still bring off successful raids from time to time and carry off a good deal of loot before the authorities intervene. Common-sense, the sentinel, is frequently asleep at his post and forgets to utter the warning cry, "Ex nihilo nail fit."

The troops that attack Snob-gate are the best turned-out regiments in the army. They are made up of Discriminating Men and Smart Women, of Typists who Marry the Boss, of Men who can Judge Whisky blindfold and Hostesses who kowtow to give their Patties that Air of Distinction. They offer Luxury Goods under – the brand of the Life Beautiful; and perhaps the worst that can be said of them is that their notion of Beauty is trivial. The finest Snob-assault I ever saw with my eyes was the advertisement of a firm of American morticians in the pre-Slump era: "Why lay your loved ones in the cold ground? Let us electro-plate them in gold or silver."

Sayles added:

> The advertising writer has to harden his heart, preserve his sense of humour and remind himself that, however loudly he shouts and however exaggerated his statements, he will be lucky if one-tenth of what he says is heard or the hundredth part of it attended to.

Advertising told some unlikely truths because anybody

> who wants to know what our national weaknesses are, has only to study the advertisement columns of the daily Press. There he will find them all, reduced to their simplest elements, decked out in whatever motley is in the mode: the truth about ourselves and the name by which we are agreed to call it. Advertising is here a safer guide than books or the theatre or the editorials or the news; for a book may enjoy a succes d'estime disproportionate to its influence, a play may be artificially nursed or flop, an editor may have a private axe

to grind, and the news may be inspired from some prejudiced source; but the advertiser looks for immediate cash returns and he dare not make a mistake.

She advised people to read the claims advertisers made with care, observing both what is said and what is omitted. Those who are not bothered about formal English have only themselves to blame if the advertising copywriter uses his mastery of words and syntax to mislead them. Caveat emptor.

> The advertisement columns of the daily Press allow us to find out 'the truth about ourselves and the name by which we are agreed to call it. Advertising is here a safer guide than books or the theatre or the editorials or the news; for a book may enjoy a succes d'estime disproportionate to its influence, a play may be artificially nursed or flop, an editor may have a private axe to grind, and the news may be inspired from some prejudiced source; but the advertiser looks for immediate cash returns and he dare not make a mistake.

> And just because he dare not make a mistake, the advertiser's influence is less evil than it might appear. By much shouting, he draws attention to himself; his goods are branded; his reputation is in the long run his livelihood. An anonymous purveyor may sand his sugar or put paper in the soles of the shoes he sells; but if the advertiser of branded goods does so, then every time his distinctive name-block appears in print the disillusioned public will grit its teeth and get cold feet. His victims will talk; his bad name will be bandied about, and he may as well hang himself at once.'

In his classic 1952 study, *The Hidden Persuaders* Vance Packard echoed Sayers stating a society where consumption is artificially stimulated in a society based on waste and trash.

The temptation to weave her knowledge of advertising into a mystery was irresistible and the title witty.

Murder Must Advertise

Death Bredon, actually Wimsey in disguise, joins Pym's Publicity Ltd as a junior copywriter. His predecessor Victor Dean fell down the office's iron spiral staircase and died. In the dead man's desk Bredon discovers an unfinished letter to Mr Pym, telling him that something "undesirable" has been going on in the office. Wimsey discovers the agency is being used in a plot to supply cocaine and that one of Pym's major clients runs a newspaper advertisement every Friday morning. The first letter of the headline is being used to indicate the pub where cocaine is supplied that week. Wimsey is sure that the manager Tallboy killed Dean. On the night of the next drug deal, Tallboy comes to Wimsey's flat to confess. He says that he was sucked into the scheme with an innocent-sounding story and the offer of money, but he soon became trapped. Dean found out and was blackmailing him. Tallboy then killed Dean making it look like an accident.

The end echoes the end of The Murder of Roger Ackroyd. *Wanting to spare his wife and child, Tallboy suggests he kill himself. Wimsey looks out of the window and has an alternative: Tallboy must leave, on foot, without looking behind him. Both know that the gang's killers are waiting because he has given enough information for the police to finally round them up.*

As in so many of the books, in the end, justice is done.

In her detective novels, Sayers had no truck with evil, but she did much more than write those. She published her last detective novel *A Busman's Holiday* in 1937. By then Wimsey and Harriett are happily married and have children but solve a case together.

After that Sayers concentrated on theology where her views of evil were more nuanced. Two works are memorable. *The Devil to Pay* is a reworking of the Faust story as a play. She also wrote a 12-play radio cycle, *The Man Born to Be King*, where Jesus is very human. In 1941 "personifying the godhead" was something of an outrage. Some listeners complained that such blasphemies caused the fall of Singapore; others said that if the plays weren't taken off the air Australia would be next and there would be no more test matches.

Her very human Christ knows Judas intends to betray him and makes a last attempt to save Judas from himself. All the characters, good and evil, are handled skilfully. The disciples own up to everyday facts and emotions. Judas is the wheeler and dealer, the epitome of all politicians, the opportunistic egotist. At the end, in his moment of tortured self-awareness, he recognises how many men there are in the world like him, "in love with suffering, because I wanted to see him [Jesus] suffer. I wanted to believe him guilty, because I could not endure his innocence."

The Lord Chamberlain, who then censored all productions, took a more Christian view one might say. There could be no blasphemy as no audience was present to witness some strutting actor impersonating Christ.

Sayers was also fascinated with the psychology of creation. *The Mind of the Maker* identifies the Trinity of Father, Son and Holy Spirit with the three stages of creation: the conception or idea; the energy; and the power over (or awareness of) the audience.

The *Christian World* enthused.

In *The Mind of the Maker*, one of her most profound works, Sayers contends that the creative process in art works in ways that correspond to the dynamic relation among the three Persons of the Trinity in Christian theology – and that the activity of one illuminates the activity of the other.

Given that Sayers had been such a success in advertising it is perhaps not surprising that even management books latched on to that as in the software management book *The Mythical Man-Month* which praised *The Mind of the Maker* for dividing:

> creative activity into three stages: the idea, the implementation, and the interaction. A book, then, or a computer, or a program comes into existence first as an ideal construct, built outside time and space, but complete in the mind of the author. It is realized in time and space, by pen, ink, and paper, or by wire, silicon, and ferrite. The creation is complete when someone reads the book, uses the computer, or runs the program, thereby interacting with the mind of the maker. This description, which Miss Sayers uses to illuminate not only human creative activity but also the Christian doctrine of the Trinity, will help us in our present task.

Sayers died in 1971. The subject of the next chapter, Anthony Berkeley Cox, was one of the most influential detective writers of the 1920s and 1930s. However, he had long dwindled into silence by the time Sayers died.

Chapter 9

Theories of learning and the rise of behaviourism

The 1920s and the work of Anthony Berkeley, the innovator who seized up

The late 1920s and early 1930s also saw the irresistible rise of behaviourism which claimed that psychologists should focus on observable behaviour. Clark Hull and B.F. Skinner were the most important proponents of those ideas.

In 1929, Clark Hull began work at Yale University, where he taught a psychological test and measurement course. Because he loved the mathematical portion of the course, he changed the class to aptitude testing. Hull had studied Pavlov's idea of conditional reflexes, and Watson's behaviourism – and both influenced him.

The image we have of classical conditioning is a dog. Dog gets a neutral signal before a naturally occurring reflex. Pavlov let the dog hear a neutral tone; the naturally occurring reflex was salivating in response to food. By associating the neutral stimulus with the environmental stimulus (food), the sound of the tone alone could produce the salivation response.

First, the unconditioned stimulus (UCS) results in an unconditioned response (UCR). For example, presenting food (the UCS) naturally and automatically triggers a salivation response (the UCR). As with dogs so with humans. For example, when you smell one of your favourite foods, you may immediately feel very hungry. In this example, the smell of the food is the unconditioned stimulus.

During the second phase of the classical conditioning process, the previously neutral stimulus is repeatedly paired with the unconditioned stimulus. As a result, an association between the previously neutral stimulus and the UCS is formed.

At this point, the once-neutral stimulus becomes known as the conditioned stimulus. Suppose that when you smelled your favourite food, you also heard the sound of a whistle. The whistle has

DOI: 10.4324/9780429344664-9

nothing to do with the smell of the food but, if the sound of the whistle is paired many times with the smell, the whistle would eventually trigger the conditioned response.

Once the association has been made between the UCS and the CS, presenting the conditioned stimulus alone will come to evoke a response even without the unconditioned stimulus. The resulting response is known as the conditioned response (CR). So you hear the whistle and the appetite is whetted.

Hull dedicated himself to perfecting his own theory of learning.

By 1930, he came to several conclusions of which the first was that psychology was a true natural science. The second was that being a science its primary laws could be expressed by equations. This does not apply to all sciences but in their wish, going back to Wundt, to be seen as pukka as physicists forgot geologists among others did not find that much use for equations.

Hull worked mainly with animals, but then his work took an unexpected turn – and one relevant to detection. He became curious about suggestion and hypnosis. There had been interest in hypnosis since Mesmer. Gauld's *A History of Hypnosis* examines in detail the work of William Esdaile who used hypnosis to anaesthetise patients in the 1840s. Esdaile is forgotten because it was easier to use ether. The Society of Psychical Research also studied hypnosis, but no one looked at the subject very scientifically til Hull became interested and he put a disturbed student into a trance.

Hull's *Hypnosis and Suggestibility* (1933) showed that hypnosis is not related to sleep and said, "the whole concept of sleep when applied to hypnosis obscures the situation." He argued that hypnosis is the opposite of sleep because he found that hypnotised subjects gave responses linked to alertness rather than lethargy. Some even felt that hypnotism made them more alert and sensitive, but this was never proven to be a significant result. Hull examined the apparently extravagant claims of hypnotists, who often boasted hypnosis made for extraordinary improvements in cognition.

Hull showed that hypnotic states and waking states are the same, besides a few simple differences. One was that subjects in hypnotic states respond to suggestions more readily than when awake and that they could better remember events that had happened far in their past. In a few detective novels, witnesses are hypnotised to get them to recall better.

Hull showed the reality of some classical phenomena such as mentally induced pain reduction and apparent inhibition of memory. However, these effects could be achieved without hypnosis but rather as a result of suggestion and motivation.

Hull's work in hypnosis quickly encountered resistance. The medical school's concern over the dangers of hypnosis caused him to stop his research. Conformity mattered in the 1930s. Carl Rogers, who devised humanist psychotherapy, stopped work on children who claimed to have been sexually abused because his colleagues disapproved.

The link between hypnosis and the whodunnit was a century old by 1930 when *Death by Suggestion: An Anthology of 19th and Early 20th-Century Tales of Hypnotically Induced Murder, Suicide, and Accidental Death* (2018) edited by Donald K. Hartman was published. It gathered 22 short stories from the 19th and early 20th centuries where hypnotism is used to cause death – deliberately or by accident. Revenge is often a motive, but the tales also have characters who die because they have a suicide wish, or they need to kill an abusive or unwanted spouse, or they just really enjoy inflicting pain on others.

The interest in mystery death by hypnosis has not waned. Gyles Brandreth's popular Oscar Wilde series is an example. At a party for the elite of London society, a beautiful young duchess is found dead in a most un-Victorian manner: half nude, abused, with two puncture wounds in her throat. To prevent scandal the prince of Wales – he whose skull was dodgy – asks Oscar Wilde to find out who killed the lady; Oscar, however, is distracted by a young actor who claims to be a vampire. Arthur Conan Doyle and Bram Stoker help Oscar investigate. He delves into the dark underbelly of Victorian society: night clubs, opium dens, lunatic asylums and graveyards where men claim to know creatures of the night.

B.F. Skinner

Behaviourism has influenced detective stories perhaps most in the police procedural which tracks how the police behave. To understand this, a look at Skinner's work is necessary. He explained to me in two interviews in the 1970s, and I met his daughter later when I wrote a book on great psychologists as parents. She told me he had been a wonderful father.

After Watson had to resign from Johns Hopkins as a result of a divorce, Skinner developed his ideas – and added many of his own. He believed that it was not really necessary to look at internal thoughts and motivations to explain behaviour. He was influenced by the work of psychologist Edward Thorndike. According to his law of effect actions that are followed by desirable outcomes are more likely to be repeated, while those followed by undesirable outcomes are less likely to be repeated.

Operant conditioning showed that when lab rats press a lever when a green light is on, they receive a food pellet as a reward. When they press the lever when a red light is on, they receive a mild electric shock. Not being dumb they learn to press the lever when the green light is on and avoid the red light.

Operant conditioning is not complex as an idea. Actions that are followed by reinforcement will be strengthened and more likely to occur again in the future. If you tell a funny story in class and everybody laughs, you will probably be more likely to tell that story again in the future. If you raise your hand to ask a question and your teacher praises you, you will be more likely to raise your hand the next time you have a question or comment. Because the behaviour was followed by reinforcement, or a desirable outcome, the preceding action is strengthened.

The reverse is true. Actions that result in punishment or undesirable consequences will be weakened and less likely to occur again. If you tell the same story again in another class but nobody laughs, you will be less likely to repeat the story again in the future. If you shout out an answer in class and your teacher scolds you, then you might be less likely to interrupt the class again.

Skinner was creative. As a boy, he invented different devices. He put these skills to work during his studies on operant conditioning. He created a device known as an operant conditioning chamber, often referred to today as a Skinner box. The chamber could hold a small animal, such as a rat or pigeon. The box also contained a bar or key that the animal could press in order to receive a reward.

Skinner also wrote two novels which illustrated how his kind of psychology could improve the world.

Walden Two is not a mystery but a utopia. It is a place for achieving self-actualisation in a community which is committed to the virtues of self-reliance. Skinner argued that free will is weak compared to how environmental conditions shape behaviour.

In the novel, Professor Burris is a university instructor of psychology, who is approached by two young men. They are veterans of the 1945 war and, intrigued by utopian ideas, want to meet an old acquaintance of Burris, T.E. Frazier who in the 1930s started a community. Frazier invites them all to stay for several days to experience life in his utopia. Frazier, a smug, talkative and colourful character, guides his visitors around Walden Two and explains how it works. There are rewards but fewer punishments. A wide range of intellectual topics is talked about including behaviour modification, the common good, free will, determinism, fascism and communism.

Walden Two boasts of practices which individualistic America thinks weird. Children are raised communally, families are non-nuclear, free affection is the norm and personal expressions of thanks are taboo. Skinner offers a "Walden Code," a guideline for self-control techniques which encourages members to credit all individual and other achievements to the larger community. Counsellors are also available to supervise behaviour and assist members with better understanding and following the Code.

Defending the virtues of democracy, one of the students finally confronts Frazier accusing him of despotism. Frazier rebuts, on the contrary, that the vision for Walden Two is as a place safe from all forms of despotism, even the "despotism of democracy."

Skinner published a follow-up to *Walden Two* in *News From Nowhere, 1984*. In it, Eric Blair lives in the community who seeks out and meets Frazier, confessing he is really George Orwell who wrote *1984*. By the time Skinner published his book Orwell had died which gave Skinner the freedom to imagine Blair and Frazier discussing the utopia. Blair/Orwell is impressed by Walden Two's "lack of any institutionalized government, religion, or economic system," a state of affairs that embodied "the dream of 19th-century anarchism."

Orwell is oddly relevant to the theme of his book as he wrote a famous essay, *The Decline of the English Murder*. Orwell appreciated the books of Conan Doyle and Austin Freeman. The year before he died Orwell wrote to a friend asking if she remembered their shared enthusiasm for Freeman's detective books. Freeman was one of the founders of an odd club.

The Detection Club

Its 26 writers included G.K. Chesterton and two doctors including Sayers' co-author Robert Eustace, four veterans of military intelligence and a chemistry professor. Its members were supposed to have the highest standards and keep to certain rules. They had to promise their detectives would

> well and truly detect the crimes presented to them using those wits which it may please you to bestow upon them and not placing reliance on nor making use of Divine Revelation, Feminine Intuition, Mumbo Jumbo, Jiggery-Pokery, Coincidence, or Act of God?

The club members enjoyed playing with the conventions. They wrote *The Floating Admiral* where each of the authors contributed a chapter leaving the next author to carry on the plot. You could imagine the residents of Walden Two collaborating on just such an enterprise. The club repeated the conceit in *Ask a Policeman* where a policeman is the last person one should ask as the constabulary was club-brained at best. Ignoring any copyright issues, Sayers let Gladys Mitchell write a Wimsey story, for example. It was all good fun.

The iconoclast

Berkeley changed the rules of the detective novel. He became determined to make the detective novel more psychological for a number of reasons. His childhood left him feeling he was not as smart and not as loved as his brother and sister.

Berkeley's father was a doctor who invented an X-ray machine that made it possible to detect shrapnel, which was very useful in the 1914 war. His mother's ancestors included an Earl of Monmouth and a smuggler, who happened to be called Francis Iles. Berkeley would use that name as the author of three of his books.

Berkeley read Classics at Oxford, but he only took a third-class degree. It seems likely this added to his sense of inferiority. His brother got a first. Perhaps because of that, he also did his best to hide biographical details, but he put many of these in his books, especially in his last *As for the Woman*. Its main character Alan is an Oxford graduate, the oldest of three children who feels unequal to his sister, a musician and his brother. In real life, Berkeley's sister was not just a good musician but also notorious as she lived with a man who was not her husband. His younger brother Stephen became a well-known mathematician.

In *As for the Woman*, Alan has literary ambitions, but he overhears his mother dismiss his teenage poetry as "empty pretentious nonsense." Berkeley's own mother was very critical of him. Her attitude, hardly that of devoted maternal love, affected his relationships with women. He lusted after them, but they frightened him. He avoided too much intimacy and was something of a curmudgeon. He gave the impression that he disliked the whole sex. And it was not just women. He confided to another member of the Detection Club, Christiana Brand, that there "was not a soul in the world he did not cordially dislike."

Berkeley served in the First World War but was gassed which affected his health for the rest of his life. In 1917, he married Margaret Farrar who was 19 years old; he was just two years older. He made his detective Sheringham say,

> I never think a first marriage ought to count. One's so busy learning how to be married at all that one can't help acquiring a kind of resentment against one's partner in error. And once resentment has crept in the thing's finished.

Like many returning soldiers, Berkeley found it hard to adjust to peacetime. He came to London and worked briefly at many jobs – farming, property management and what he called "social work," a profession that had hardly been invented at the time. He also took part in amateur dramatics perhaps because acting allowed him to mask his true self. He played the major domo in his own comic opera *The Family Witch*. Berkeley was rich as his family owned a number of properties, so he never had to write for money as Christie and Sayers did at the start of their careers.

Though his mother had a low opinion of his teenage poetry, Berkeley still had literary ambitions. He contributed to Punch. One of his pieces was a spoof of a Conan Doyle story written in the style of Wodehouse. Six years after the war ended, Berkeley published a real detective novel, but he did so anonymously. He may have been anxious about the reaction it would get. He was surprised by how well it sold.

The Layton Court Mystery (1925) introduced his fallible detective Roger Sheringham. The most direct influence was E.C. Bentley, who had written the best seller *Trent's Last Case* more than a decade earlier. Like Bentley, Berkeley decided his detective would be no Sherlock Holmes, explaining in the dedication:

I have tried to make the gentleman who eventually solves the mystery as nearly as possible as he might be expected to do in real life. That is to say, he is very far removed from a sphinx and he does make a mistake or two occasionally. I have never believed very much in those hawk-eyed, tight-lipped gentry who pursue their silent and inexorable way straight to the heart of things without ever once overbalancing or turning aside after false goals.

Berkeley was an assiduous student of real crime. One of the cases that inspired him was that of Dr Crippen who killed his wife and remains famous because Scotland Yard sent a telegram to New York to make sure Crippen was arrested when he landed. Crippen's psychology baffled Berkeley, however, who argued "one does not remain gentle and kindly for 48 years and then reveal one is a fiend." In fact, Crippen was a good example of sex being a motive. He got rid of his wife to marry a younger woman.

Berkeley's second novel *The Wychford Poisoning Case* (1926) used elements of the late 19th-century Maybrick murder in Liverpool. Maybrick was a successful cotton trader but also a drug addict. His young wife Florence took a lover, so Maybrick did the same and had children by his mistress. When Maybrick died in 1889 the police suspected Florence had poisoned him. She was found guilty but did not hang as Queen Victoria pardoned her.

Berkeley dedicated the book to E.M. Delafield, a woman he had an intense but perhaps not sexual relationship with. He told her he hoped that she would

recognise the attempt I have made to substitute for the materialism of the usual crime-puzzle of fiction those psychological values which are ... the basis of the universal interest in the far more absorbing criminological dramas of real life. In other words, I have tried to write what might be described as a psychological detective story.

Berkeley added that he was interested to compare these "engines of the human chassis with my own, so like and so unlike."

Berkeley enjoyed the playful spirit of the Detection Club. He was happy to let Lord Peter Wimsey comment on the fallible detective in *Have His Carcase*:

There's the Roger Sheringham method, for instance. You prove elaborately and in detail that A did the murder; then you give the story one final shake, twist it around a fresh corner, and find the real murderer is B – the person you suspected first and lost sight of ...

In 1927, Berkeley decided to publish a novel not under his own name but that of his ancestor Frances Iles. He was trying to carve out a new voice, perhaps even a new identity, with a story that explored more complex psychological themes.

Berkeley broke one of the rules of the detective novel because he decided not to give readers any puzzle by revealing the killer at the very start. He certainly could write an arresting opening. In his first book, he said,

it was not until several weeks after he had decided to murder his wife that Dr Bickleigh took any serious steps in the matter. Murder is a serious business. The slightest slip may be disastrous. Dr Bickleigh had no intention of risking disaster.

Dr. Bickleigh is fed up with his domineering wife, Julia, and hopes to marry a younger woman, Madeleine. Julia resists that, so he uses his medical knowledge to murder her. His method is a devious and some would say unusually cruel one: he slowly feeds her a chemical which gives her blinding headaches. She takes painkillers so that she apparently dies of an accidental overdose of opium. He appears to get away with it, but one person who suspects the truth is Madeleine, who marries another man, and some people in the local community wrongly suspect that Julia committed suicide because of problems in their marriage. As Dr. Bickleigh realises that Madeleine suspects what has happened, he attempts to poison her and her new husband; they survive, but this leads the authorities to become suspicious about the earlier death of Julia. Her body is exhumed, and Dr. Bickleigh is put on trial for her murder.

The New York Times called the book a "fine psychological study of a distorted mind." *The English Review* praised it as "psychologically extremely good."

Berkeley cannot be understood without understanding his romantic view of England and the monarchy. In 1936, when Edward VIII was under pressure to abandon his plan to marry Mrs

Simpson, Berkeley pursued a bizarre campaign to save King Edward VIII from the clutches of the American divorcee.

In the next novel, *Before the Fact*, which Berkeley wrote under the name of Frances Iles, again he provided an arresting opening. "Some women give birth to murderers, some go to bed with them, and some marry them. Lina Aysgarth had lived with her husband for nearly eight years before she realized that she was married to a murderer."

Berkeley's last novel *As for the Woman* (1939) was judged "frank to the point of indecency" by J.D. Beresford in *The Manchester Guardian*. In this story, Alan Littlewood becomes infatuated with the wife of a doctor. Berkeley's usual publishers found it too "sadistic." When another publisher took it on, they trumpeted on the jacket that the book

> is not intended to thrill. It is no more, and at the same time no less, than a sincere attempt to depict the love of a young, inexperienced man for a woman much older than himself, with all its idealism, its heart burnings, and its inevitable disappointments.

At the end of the book Mrs. Pawle rejects Alan – she had never intended to leave her husband anyway – but also teases and even endangers him. She sends him out wearing a dress "which might earn him a prison sentence" because it made him a suspect in the murder. When Alan asks how she could have let that happen she replies, "It was your penance for our sin." Her penance is having to continue to live with her husband. She warns Alan not to be vindictive, but she can't help saying that while her husband Fred took her betrayal seriously but "not so seriously as if you'd been a real man." Hurt, Alan asks her if he is a hermaphrodite.

On his way back to London Alan cries. "Life was unbearable with that protective shell stripped from his secret mind and the true self exposed in all its raw ugliness."

Fred had finished him.

Fred had destroyed his soul.

The failure of *As for the Woman* hurt Berkeley deeply, and he never published another novel. H.R. Keating, the author of some fine mysteries set in India, called *As for the Woman* one of the key texts in the history of crime fiction.

As far as I have been able to find out Berkeley never met George Orwell which is a shame as they have some similarities in their romantic view of England. Orwell's *Coming Up for Air* has as its "hero" a commercial traveller who returns to the village where he was born. Everything has changed. The novel is a lament for a disappearing England. Orwell might be a socialist and thought the aristocracy a menace, but he loved the Englishness of England, its bitter beer and football crowds with mild knobbly faces and bad teeth. Orwell feared fascism and seems to have thought the working class would never stand for jackboots and ludicrous militaristic. Berkeley's *O England* of 1940 suggests he shared these views and reminds one how profoundly English the classic detective books of the 1920s were. One should remember that only one detective was not English, the lord of the grey cells, Hercule Poirot. Only a foreigner could possibly boast so much of his brain power.

> When you come back to England from any foreign country, you have immediately the sensation of breathing a different air. Even in the first few minutes dozens of small things conspire to give you this feeling. The beer is bitterer, the coins are heavier, the grass is greener, the advertisements are more blatant. The crowds in the big towns, with their mild knobby faces, their bad teeth and gentle manners, are different from a European crowd. Then the vastness of England swallows you up, and you lose for a while your feeling that the whole nation has a single identifiable character.

But talk to foreigners, read foreign books or newspapers, and you are brought back to the same thought. Yes, there *is* something distinctive and recognisable in English civilisation. It is a culture as individual as that of Spain. It is somehow bound up with solid breakfasts and gloomy Sundays, smoky towns and winding roads, green fields and red pillar-boxes. It has a flavour of its own.

Berkeley said he was hoping to provoke debate, and persuade others to support his campaign, and also announced that he was to produce a follow-up. But there seems to have been widespread apathy about his plans, and he lost heart both with his fiction and nonfiction. He took to reviewing crime novels and encouraged Ruth Rendell and P.D. James.

In the 1940s, Alfred Hitchcock transformed *Before the Fact* into a famous movie starring Cary Grant, *Suspicion*. Even this success did not tempt Berkeley to pick up his pen again.

In *Elusion Aforethought: The Life and Writing of Anthony Berkeley Cox* (1996), Malcolm J. Turnbull speculates that punitive income tax rates also discouraged Berkeley from writing as did the failure of both of his marriages. These all turned him into a disappointed even sour man. Christianna Brand, a near-neighbour in London and a fellow Detection Club member, wrote that he had been "charming, urbane and ... perhaps the cleverest of us all," but added that he became "rude, overbearing, and really horrid. And mean!" Poor health also added to his problems. The American critic James Sandoe, who met him in the 1960s, said that "his heart was weak but his spirit gallant." Certainly, Edwards wrote: "Nobody has ever done ironic ingenuity better than Anthony Berkeley."

Chapter 10

Attachment theory and the work of John Bowlby

Psychology between 1930 and 1945 and the novels of Gladys Mitchell

Gladys Mitchell was considered the equal of Christie and Sayers in the 1930s and even dared to parody Christie in *The Mystery of a Butcher's Shop* (1929) and *The Saltmarsh Murders* (1932). Mitchell has had a new lease of life as *The Mrs Bradley Mysteries* based on her books which is a TV series starring the late Diana Rigg. Rigg makes Mrs Bradley very glamorous but tends to downplay the fact that she is a psychoanalyst.

The golden age of detective fiction was pre post-truth as it were, when lies were simple. Even not truth was not simple though. Freud, of course, thought patients lied both consciously and unconsciously. There is no evidence that he ever met or corresponded with Gladys Mitchell but of all the detective authors she was perhaps most in his debt.

Gladys Mitchell worked as a teacher all her life and lived with a woman for some 40 years. She had a feel for the bizarre and was interested in witchcraft. She studied Freud thoroughly and wrote a novel every year from 1928 through to her death in 1983.

She also wrote poetry. Freud – and Bowlby – would have approved of one of her poems which echoed the view that the reasons for murder lie in the killer's childhood. A killer was a child who had been maimed by lack of love and so turned to violence. He/she was not a murdering ape like the ourang-outang in Poe's classic book.

In Mitchell's first novel the killer was certainly not a murderous ape. *Speedy Death* published in 1929 introduced Mrs Bradley, a qualified psychoanalyst (though we never learn who she trained under) and an amateur detective who was never shy of using Freudian insights. *Speedy Death* broke the rules perhaps even more than any of Berkeley's books.

DOI: 10.4324/9780429344664-10

The setting is a country house, and especially the bathroom. Everard Mountjoy is found dead in the bath. Mountjoy was engaged to Eleanor Bing and appeared to be male, but when the pathologist examined his body he turned out to be a woman. This is yet another example of how comfortable authors were with sexual ambiguity.

Later Eleanor, who Mountjoy deceived, is "framed in the doorway and looking the picture of maniacal fury." One can hardly blame her. The fact that he is not male has made a perfect fool of her. She is holding an enormous carving knife. When she laughed the blood froze in the veins of the two witnesses to the scene.

"She's mad," one of them says sanely enough. They still manage to overpower her.

Before the Mountjoy gender debacle, Eleanor was a rather correct young woman. Now she began to shout, "a stream of the most foul and abominable filth which ever disgraced the name of language." When one of the men tries to put his hand over her mouth, she bites him.

Luckily Mrs Bradley enters at this point and tells Eleanor she is being foolish and gives her a powerful sedative. Eleanor does not resist. Mrs Bradley then locks her in her own bedroom and tucks her in like one would a frightened child. When the men want to know what she is suffering from, Mrs Bradley replies, "Bad case of nervous breakdown." The men comment it's a surprise, recent events have not turned them all into "gibbering maniacs."

In the morning, Eleanor herself is found dead and her body is also in the bathroom. A Scotland Yard officer, who goes by the not-subtle name of Inspector Boring, suspects Mrs Bradley because he is suspicious of her psychoanalytic expertise. Though his chief constable urges caution, Boring charges her.

At the trial Mrs Bradley's son, who is a well-known barrister, defends her. She pleads not guilty. The evidence against her is weak, he argues, and Mrs Bradley is acquitted.

Afterwards, she admits to her son that she did commit the murder, but for an unusual reason. She believed Eleanor was dangerous as well as mad. She might have had cause to kill Mountjoy, but she would kill again because she got a taste for it. The only way to protect society, Mrs Bradley believed, was to dispose of her. In *Curtains*, Christie let Poirot murder for the same reason. One critic who liked the book said, the only plot detail not answered is why old Mountjoy decided to masquerade as a man in the first place.

Mitchell and Mrs Bradley would have been familiar with one of the key developments of 1940 psychology.

In 1944, the psychoanalyst John Bowlby argued that children who were separated from their mothers were more likely to become juvenile delinquents. He suggested the roots of emotional disorders and delinquency could be found in early attachment-related experiences, specifically separations from, or inconsistent or harsh treatment by, mothers. He then built a complex and influential theory of attachment.

Bowlby formed a working relationship with a very talented empirically oriented researcher, Mary Ainsworth. Her observations, first in Uganda (Ainsworth, 1967) and later her creation of the *Strange Situation* (Ainsworth, Blehar, Waters, & Wall, 1978), made it possible to classify individual differences in infant attachment security (and insecurity). In the *StrangeSituation*, a child is placed in an unfamiliar environment. How the child copes reflects his/her history.

Children grow and thrive in the context of close and dependable relationships that provide love and nurturance, security, responsive interaction and encouragement for exploration. Without at least one such relationship, development is disrupted, and the consequences can be severe and long-lasting. The insecure child gets frozen or scared.

Years after Ainsworth's *Strange Situation*, Mary Main and colleagues found that a parent's "state of mind with respect to attachment" predicted his/her infant's pattern of attachment. Since the 1980s, there has been much research that has supported Bowlby's (1979) belief that attachment is a process that characterizes humans "from the cradle to the grave."

And Bowlby has been backed by Harlow's animal experiments. He gave young rhesus monkeys a choice between two different "mothers." One was made of soft terrycloth but provided no food. The other was made of wire but provided nourishment from an attached baby bottle.

Harlow removed young monkeys from their natural mothers a few hours after birth and left them to be "raised" by these mother surrogates. The experiment demonstrated that the baby monkeys spent significantly more time with their cloth mother than with their wire mother. The infant monkeys went to the wire mother only for food but preferred to spend their time with the soft, comforting cloth mother when they were not eating. Harlow concluded that affection was the primary force behind the need for closeness.

Harlow used a "strange situation" technique similar to the one created by Ainsworth. Young monkeys were allowed to explore a room either in the presence of their surrogate mother or in her absence.

Monkeys who were with their cloth mother would use her as a secure base to explore the room. When the surrogate mothers were removed from the room, the effects were dramatic. The young monkeys no longer had their secure base for exploration and would often freeze up, crouch, rock, scream and cry.

The plight of abandoned children is a frequent subject in fairy tales, and in some detective novels, they come back and wreak revenge as in a number of Agatha Christie stories. Mitchell placed her *When Last I Died* in an institution for delinquents, and most of them had suffered bad parenting indeed – and wanted revenge. In examining this seriously, Mitchell offered readers a very entertaining introduction to Freudian ideas.

J'Accuse

Despite the fact that they were often both intelligent and popular, in 1946, the literary critic Edmund Wilson blasted the detective novel in the *New Yorker*. He was puzzled that "the spell of the detective story that has been felt by T. S. Eliot and Paul Elmer More but which I seem to be unable to feel?"

Wilson was especially baffled by the fact the author of *The Wasteland* could be bothered to review detective novels for his literary journal *The Criterion*. These reviews made clear Eliot's passion for detective fiction and his attempts to define the genre as it was evolving as Christie, Sayers and Gladys Mitchell enjoyed experimenting with the form. None of that impressed Wilson who sniped:

> As a department of imaginative writing, it looks to me completely dead. The spy story may only now be realizing its poetic possibilities, as the admirers of Graham Greene contend; and the murder story that exploits psychological horror is an entirely different matter. But the detective story proper bore its really fine fruit in the middle of the 19th century, when Poe

communicated to M. Dupin (his detective) something of his own ratiocinative intensity and when Dickens invested his plots with a social and moral significance that made the final solution of the mystery a revelatory symbol of something that the author wanted seriously to say. Yet the detective story has kept its hold; had even, in the two decades between the great wars, become more popular than ever before.

Wilson offered "a deep reason for this. The world during those years was ridden by an all-pervasive guilt." The detective novel pointed the fingers conclusively at who was to blame.

> Who had committed the original crime and who was going to commit the next one? – that murder which always, in the novels, occurs at an unexpected moment, when the investigation is well under way, which may happen, as in one of the Nero Wolfe stories, right in the great detective's office.

Rex Stout's Nero Wolfe is an eccentric detective. He does not allow anyone to call him by his first name and hardly ever leaves his New York home. He drinks beer morning to night and spends most of his day in his greenhouse. His assistant brings him the details of the cases they are investigating. Wolfe sits and thinks and solves. Wolfe has a pathological aversion to the company of women. He can't stand being touched by anyone.

In his *J'Accuse*, Wilson fires on.

> Everybody is suspected in turn, and the streets are full of lurking agents whose allegiances we cannot know. Nobody seems guiltless, nobody seems safe; and then, suddenly, the murderer is spotted, and – relief! – he is not, after all, a person like you or me. He is a villain – known to the trade as George Gruesome – and he has been caught by an infallible Power, the supercilious and omniscient detective, who knows exactly how to fix the guilt.

Wilson was so brutal one almost wonders if he tried to write a detective novel and failed.

I explained earlier that Berkeley re-wrote a *Sherlock Holmes* story in the style of P.G. Wodehouse. I had wanted to include Wodehouse who created a marvellous demented psychiatrist Sir

Roderick Glossop who diagnoses Wooster as a kleptomaniac, but Wodehouse was hardly a detective writer.

Dear Reader,

nevertheless, indulge me in a small fantasy.

My fantasy imagines an encounter between two brains of the highest calibre in fiction. The immaculate butler Jeeves says: "May I serve you a sole meuniere, Mr Poirot?"

"Non mon ami. I detest the fish."

"Your little grey cells need nourishment, sir," says Jeeves as he dishes up. "Allow me to serve the sole a la facon Wooster."

The recipe remains a mystery, but Poirot enjoyed it with a glass of Chablis, and a fine liqueur. Georges Simenon, easily the greatest of all the detective authors, created a detective who was very different from Poirot in almost every respect. But both Poirot and Maigret grasped the psychology of the criminal profoundly.

Chapter 11

Psychoanalysis and psychiatry from 1930 to 1960

Georges Simenon and the intellectual egos of Sartre and Lacan

In his 60s, Georges Simenon gave an interview to four doctors in which he said,

> I have spent my life struggling between reason and the unconscious because my work is done by the unconscious. If I knew myself too well I don't believe I could write. The day when I became rational I would lose the precision of my subconscious.

Simenon echoes Goethe's remark which Freud often quoted: "If I knew myself I'd run away." When he was interviewed by the doctors, Simenon admitted, "It is quite extraordinary, I'm afraid of understanding myself but I want to."

Admired as they are, none of the British detective writers is seen as a truly great writer. Simenon is. Apart from his Maigret books, he wrote a number of black novels as well as *Letter to My Judge*. The latter is fiction but feels very autobiographical.

Simenon was born in Liege in Belgium. His mother was a devout Catholic, and he became an altar boy. At school, he was usually top of his class, but hardly a model of good behaviour as he became leader of a local gang. In 1914, his headmaster asked him to see him urgently. He had bad news. He would have to abandon his studies and earn a living because his father had died. Simenon said he did not cry but felt the loss profoundly. He abandoned the idea of studying medicine.

He went to see the editor of Liege's leading paper. He must have talked well as he persuaded him to take him on as a cub reporter. For the next few years, Simenon turned out reams of copy often

DOI: 10.4324/9780429344664-11

sitting in the newsroom, writing up whatever seemed interesting that day. He reported cases in the courts and became friendly with the local police and familiar with local criminals. None of the detective writers of the golden age spent time in the neighbourhood nick.

Simenon's interest in medicine stayed with him all his life. He kept medical journals in his office including *Medicine and Hygiene*. Medicine he insisted was just a hobby, but that hobby influenced his work deeply. As Christie predated the work on false confessions Simenon wrote a short story in which he seems to have identified a psychiatric syndrome before any psychiatrists did.

Mr Monday, published in 1944, described the syndrome now known as De Clérambault's syndrome. Simenon wrote the story shortly before or simultaneously with De Clérambault's first clinical description of its symptoms.

In the story, the parents of a servant girl Olga have lodged a complaint with the police, and Maigret has gone to investigate. Olga died mysteriously while working for Dr Barion. The autopsy found that she had been four months pregnant. Dr Barion says the father of the child was his chauffeur and valet. The autopsy also revealed she had ingested rye spears, a method of murder known in the Far East. Dr Barion has discovered that a tramp who came regularly to the house on Mondays, and so was called Mr Monday, regularly brought the children cakes called religieuses; rye spears had been baked into the cakes. Olga had eaten some. Mr Monday was innocent, but Maigret learned that one of Barion's neighbours, an Englishwoman Laurence Wilfur, was obsessively in love with Barion, and had poisoned the cakes in a way that natives had used to kill her father when he was a colonial officer. She spent the rest of her days in an asylum.

The De Clerambault patient is usually a woman who believes that an important or famous person is in love with her. Goldstein (1986) corresponded with Simenon and learned that the genesis of the story came from his imagination and was not the product of research on the topic. Goldstein suggested that perhaps the syndrome should be renamed Simenon's syndrome (Goldstein, 1986).

Simenon was keen on trying to understand himself though he sometimes denied it. None of the English language detective writers gave anything like the detail he did about what impelled them to write.

To the four doctors, Simenon described a childhood habit. He was always the first person to get up in his household though he did not especially like getting up early. He admitted this was a defence mechanism because he felt guilty if he did not do so. When he was

17 and working as a cub reporter, one of his friends invited him to his home. The family owned the best wine merchants in Liege. The next day Simenon asked his friend if he should not marry his 17-year-old sister. Six months later he did just that. He admitted: "I married to protect myself from myself." It worked. It stopped him joining the local anarchist group. Without the marriage, he would have been lured into "the worst extreme actions." Writing novels was also a restraint. The discipline of writing also kept him away from dangers. When he felt he was about to commit a folly, he would go to his doctor who would ask:

"When are you starting on your next book?"
"In eight days,"
"Then it's fine," the doctor concluded.

Simenon compared writing a new book to getting a new prescription for a medicine.

The four interviewers then quoted a remark Charlie Chaplin made to Simenon. "As soon as you feel uneasy you write a book or make a film. It replaces the psychoanalyst and instead of our paying them they pay us." Simenon thought there was a good deal of truth in what Chaplin said.

Simenon read the books of the medical students at his lodgings and later read Freud and Jung. The interviewers then suggested he took more from Freud than from Jung. Simenon replied that might be correct, but that like Jung he was tempted to escape from himself. He went into a little detail. Jung had suffered greatly from his family being respectable – his father was a pastor. Simenon too had been born into a family that prized being respectable. When he was 60, he even tried to meet Jung, but he had left it too late. Jung died eight days after Simenon fixed to see him.

Simenon wrote nearly 200 books. *Maigret and the Revolver* is one of many of his novels that highlight psychology. It opens with Maigret comparing a case with a sick person whose ailments are vague, perhaps too vague to hurry to the doctor. His wife unusually plays a large part in the novel. A young man turns up at the Maigrets' flat asking to see the detective. He then disappears having stolen Maigret's revolver.

The medical details continue after the body of a politician is found in a trunk at the Gare du Nord. As the case continues, Maigret and his wife dine with Dr Pardon and his wife as well as a leading psychiatrist. Pardon turns out to be the physician of a sad man whose nickname is the Baron. The Baron suffers from anxiety and plagues his doctor with real and imagined symptoms. When Maigret discovers the Baron was seen putting a trunk in the taxi he goes to interview him. The Baron becomes paranoid and begs not to be hit when he is interviewed. The novel then discusses the question of whether the Baron is faking his symptoms. At one point, Maigret jibes that two psychiatrists can never agree.

There are splendid side characters including the Baron's ice-cold daughter and his son. Maigret eventually tracks the son to London. The Baron was helping an old lover blackmail the politician but killed him in a panic. Maigret is kind to his son and ensures he only gets a light sentence. The father is sent to an asylum.

Simenon told his interviewers that he suffered a crisis in 1930 when he had written 18 Maigret books. When writing one of his other novels *The Man Who Saw Trains Pass*, he suffered a kind of breakdown and felt that if he continued to write drawing so much on his unconscious he would end up like the German philosopher Nietzsche – mad. Simenon decided to put a brake on his descent into a kind of madness.

One of the strangest revelations of the interview was the esteem Simenon held beggars in, and that he sometimes fantasised living as one. The interviewers asked why. Simenon replied he had an uncle who was a beggar. He spent some time talking to beggars in Paris; not all of them were desperate human beings. Three or four he knew had chosen being a beggar almost as a vocation. Pascal Bruckner has commented that one of the great pleasures of reading Simenon is that his hundreds of characters are an atlas of humanity – or of the French.

On the radio station France Inter in May 2020 Bruckner compared Simenon to the 19th-century classic author Maupassant, as both their works paint a picture of a society at a particular time. Pascal points to *Letter to My Judge* as well as to *The Blue Room, the Train* and *Maigret et les braves gens*, les braves gens being decent folk.

Simenon's interest in medicine and psychology influenced his books – and one psychoanalyst seems relevant, Jacques Lacan.

Dear Reader,

An author should reveal his or her prejudices – and so.

Lacan seems obscure and narcissistic. I have tried to outline some of his key concepts because he influenced Pierre Bayard and inspired a book about murder scene investigation.

Lacan's first contribution to psychoanalytic theory was the mirror stage, which he described as "formative of the function of the 'I' as revealed in psychoanalytic experience." He claimed that

the mirror stage is a phenomenon to which I assign a twofold value. In the first place, it has historical value as it marks a decisive turning-point in the mental development of the child. In the second place, it typifies an essential libidinal relationship with the body-image.

The Ego is the result of a conflict between what one sees and what one feels, to put it simply. Lacan called this alienation. He went on to claim that at six months the baby does not have much physical coordination, but can recognise himself/herself in a mirror. The baby sees his/her image as a whole, but the baby still cannot co-ordinate his/her body. For Lacan, the wholeness of the image threatens the child with fragmentation. So the mirror stage produces tension between the subject and the image. The baby, Lacan argues, however, enjoys a moment of jubilation.

There are two problems. First, many studies show that babies do not recognise themselves in a mirror till they are 18 months old. Second, when writing my PhD I found that toddlers laugh when they saw themselves on television, but it might have been over-interpreting to call this jubilation; some of their reactions suggested surprise rather.

Freud in his *Project for a Scientific Psychology* used formulae to explain the dynamics of the mind but gave up on the attempt. Lacan too often used algebraic symbols, and they are not simple: the big Other (l'Autre) is designated A, and the little other (l'autre) is designated a. Lacan said: "the analyst must be imbued with the difference between A and a, so he can situate himself in the place of Other, and not the other." Dylan Evans explained:

1. The little other is the other who is not really other, but a reflection and projection of the Ego. It sounds I would say frivolously like "A mini me." It may sound frivolous but the great 17th philosopher, Blaise Pascal said those who mock philosophy are philosophers themselves which may justify speaking of mini-mes.
2. The big Other. "It is the mother who first occupies the position of the big Other for the child," Dylan Evans explains, "it is she

who receives the child's primitive cries" and the child has to respond.

In terms of this book, one interesting study is Henry Bond's *Lacan at the Scene.*

A Lacanian approach to murder scene investigation

What if Jacques Lacan – the brilliant and eccentric Parisian psychoanalyst – had worked as a police detective, applying his theories to solve crimes, Bond asks. This may conjure up the image of film clip starring Peter Sellers in a trench coat. Like Inspector Clouseau Lacan takes himself utterly seriously. In *Lacan at the Scene,* Henry Bond claims that the events of violent death can be more effectively unravelled with Lacan's theory of psychoanalysis than with the police's forensic tools.

Bond places Lacan at the crime scene and builds his argument through a series of crime scene photographs from the 1950s – the period when Lacan was developing his theories. It is not the horror of the ravished and mutilated corpses that draws his attention; instead, he seizes on seemingly minor details from the every day, isolating and rephotographing what at first seems insignificant: a single high-heeled shoe on a kitchen table, for example, or carefully folded clothes placed over a chair. From these mundane details, Bond builds a robust and comprehensive manual for Lacanian crime investigation that he compares to the FBI's standard-issue *Crime Classification Manual.*

It seems fitting to place Lacan's theory at a murder scene as he was usually biffing all other theorists apart from Freud. His "return to Freud" was spiced up with a radical critique of ego psychology.

The aim of psychoanalysis is to lead the analysand to recognise his/her desire. Lacan wrote in *The Ego in Freud's Theory and in the Technique of Psychoanalysis*: "… what is important is to teach the subject to name, to articulate, to bring desire into existence. The subject should come to recognize and to name her/his desire."

You imagine desire seeks to be fulfilled. Not quite according to Slavoj Zizek, the influential philosopher, who argues "desire's *raison d'être* is not to realize its goal, to find full satisfaction, but to reproduce itself as desire."

In *The Four Fundamental Concepts of Psychoanalysis,* Lacan argues that "man's desire is the desire of the Other." Some clarifications are as follows:

1. *Désir de l'Autre*, which is translated as "desire for the Other" (though could be also "desire of the Other"). The fundamental desire is the incestuous desire for the mother, the primordial Other.
2. Desire is "the desire for something else" since it is impossible to desire what one already has. The object of desire is continually deferred, which is why desire is a metonymy. A famous example is, "The pen is mightier than the sword," from Edward Bulwer Lytton's play Richelieu. This sentence has two metonyms: "Pen" stands for "the written word." And "Sword" stands for "military aggression."
3. Desire appears in the field of the Other, that is in the unconscious.

The analytic hour was good enough for Freud, but Lacan was the speedy Gonzalez of therapy. He introduced the "variable-length psychoanalytic session" which led to conflicts with the International Psychoanalytic Association; it sniped his "innovation of reducing the fifty-minute analytic hour to a Delphic seven or eight minutes (or sometimes even to a single oracular *parole* murmured in the waiting-room)" was unacceptable. Lacan's variable-length sessions lasted anywhere from a few minutes or even a few seconds to several hours.

I am tempted to write if the nothing nothings itself, as Sartre wrote, maybe the Other others itself.

Sartre – murder can be authentic

Sartre is at his most relevant to the themes in this book in his novels and plays. "Hell is other people," one of his characters says in *Huis Clos* and many killers do find other people so hellish they have to be eliminated. Philosophers are not immune from homicidal tendencies incidentally. Wittgenstein, whose dying words were "it's been a wonderful life," must have forgotten one less-than-wonderful moment; he was so annoyed by Karl Popper he hit him with a poker during a meeting of philosophers.

Sartre also studied Freud and wrote a screenplay on Freud's life which was too long but became the basis for a famous John Huston film. Sartre's philosophy asserts that we are infinitely free and that this freedom enables us to make authentic choices. No one has written a thesis comparing Sartre and Skinner, but they would have totally different accounts of a murderer. Skinner would trace the rewards and punishments which in the end made him/her a killer. Good defence lawyers often plead the background of the accused in mitigation. A lawyer who believed in Sartre would never do that because we are all free, free to kill or not to kill. Sartre presents his notion of freedom as amounting to making choices, and indeed not being able to avoid making choices.

As well as philosophy Sartre wrote plays and novels – and two involve murders. Written in 1943, Sartre's first play *Les Mouches* "The Flies" follows Electra and Orestes, as they try to avenge their father, King Agamemnon. He was murdered by their mother and her new husband. In *Les Mouches,* Orestes must take responsibility for his own hand in the murders of the book. The play explores the idea of our own guilt in the choices we make. Rejecting responsibility in the play results in characters being plagued by swarms of flies – a symbol of guilt and punishment.

Five years later *Les Mains Sales*, meaning "Dirty Hands," centred on the issues of being politically active. The assassination of a politician is at the heart of it. Hugo, a young Communist, decides to murder the party leader when he betrays the party's principles. Hugo accepts he is free to act as he wishes and get his "hands dirty" by killing. The play is often labelled "anti-Communist." Sartre himself was a Marxist and was rather romantic about politically inspired cruelty. When he met Che Guevara he declared him to be "the era's most perfect man."

In fact, Guevara was a harsh disciplinarian who sometimes shot defectors. He sent squads to track deserters. He became feared for his brutality and ruthlessness. He was also responsible for summary executions of men accused of being informers or deserters. In his diaries, Guevara described the first such execution of Eutimio Guerra, a peasant army guide who admitted treason when it was discovered he accepted the promise of 10,000 pesos for repeatedly giving away the rebel's position for attack by the Cuban air force. When asked that they "end his life quickly," Che stepped forward and shot him in the head, writing "The situation was uncomfortable for the people and for Eutimio, so I ended the problem giving him a shot with a .32 pistol in the right side of the brain, with exit orifice in the right temporal [lobe]." This matter-of-fact description suggested to one biographer a "remarkable detachment to violence" by that point in the war. Later, Guevara published an account of the incident, where he turned Eutimio's betrayal and pre-execution request that the revolution "take care of his children," into a "revolutionary parable about redemption through sacrifice." None of that bothered Sartre, it seems, however.

Simenon's fascination with psychiatry also is clear in *Maigret's Memoirs* where the detective details his own background fills in Simenon's interest in medicine. Early in the book Maigret is summoned to see his chief. A writer called Sim is also there. The chief tells Maigret that Sim is writing about the police who have usually been ridiculed in literature. Maigret agrees and reminds both men that early in his career he caught a thief outside a metro station. The thief yelled. Maigret shouted he was a policeman. The result was that the crowd fell upon him which allowed the man to escape.

Sim then explains he needs to get to know Maigret. "I don't know for what reason we did not burst out laughing," but they did not so Maigret embarked on explaining his history and motives. He was born in 1877 in central France, not far from Moulins, the only child of a farmer and his wife. When he was eight years old Maigret's mother died in childbirth. His father managed an estate of 7,500 acres, which included at least 20 small farms. His father had been better educated than most peasants and went to high school at Moulins largely because the village priest encouraged him to.

Maigret describes his father as

> very tall, very thin, his thinness emphasized by narrow trousers, bound in by leather gaiters to just below the knee. I always saw my father in leather gaiters. They were a sort of uniform for him. He wore no beard, but a long sandy moustache in which, when he came home in winter, I used to feel tiny ice-crystals when I kissed him.

Jules was sent to board at the high school in Moulins because his father was unable to take him back and forth each night, picking him up only on Saturday nights.

"I won't go so far as to say we were strangers to one another," Jules recalls, "but I had my own private life, my ambitions, my problems. He was my father, whom I loved and respected, but whom I'd given up trying to understand. And it went on like that for years."

Maigret started to study medicine in Paris and liked to try to predict the ultimate cause of death of the patients he saw. The doctors who interviewed Simenon suggested that Maigret behaved rather like a psychotherapist though he never finished his medical studies as a result of a chance meeting.

Maigret's first job was to patrol the streets in uniform.

> I wore it, not for long, for seven or eight months. As I had long legs and was very lean, very swift, strange as that may seem today, they gave me a bicycle and, in order that I might get to know Paris, where I was always losing my way, I was given the job of delivering notes to various police stations.

Maigret was soon promoted to a plainclothes position as secretary to the station officer of the Saint Georges District, a job described as being the "station officer's dog."

At this point, Xavier Guichard, a friend of his father, took Maigret under his wing and got him a job as a member of the public highways squad. He had to tramp the streets in very cheap hobnail boots. He learned about the men and women who "spend most of their nights at the police station." He learned, even more, when he was transferred to the vice squad.

Then Maigret bumped into an old friend from medical school, Felix Jubert who introduced him to Mr and Mrs Leonard and their niece, Louise. She was a "rather plump young girl with a very fresh face and a sparkle in her eyes that was lacking in her friends." It did not take long for Maigret to ask her to marry him. Simenon describes Madame Maigret as "a good housewife, always busy cooking and polishing, always fussing over her great baby of a husband."

In the books Madame Maigret brings her husband coffee every morning, always has lunch ready for him in case he returns home; she understands his bear with a sore head moods when he is struggling with a case. In the latest ITV television series, Maigret's wife sometimes helps him in his investigations. Simenon would almost certainly have disapproved totally of promoting her in this way.

Simenon married his own first wife when he was only 20 and claimed once to have slept with 10,000 women though the real number was probably just 1,200. Just! There are no sex scenes between Maigret and his wife which is ironic given Simenon's priapic nature.

When he is finally assigned to investigative detective work at the *Quai des Orfèvres*, he quickly rises in rank. At the age of 30, Maigret is transferred to the homicide squad, under Inspector Guillaume. Maigret is not blasé about his new assignment. "I could hear triumphant clarion calls ringing in my ears," he says. "The dream of my life was being realized." Running home to tell his wife the good news, he trips and falls at the door, picks himself up and nearly faints. As the most respected member of the squad, he indulges himself in the luxury of reflecting and pontificating on his job: "With all due deference to novelists," he says, "a detective is, above all, a professional. He is an *official*."

In most of the classic detective books, the policeman does not manage on his own. Japp needs Poirot; Chief Inspector Parker needs Wimsey, and Scotland Yard would often be clueless if Miss Marple were not on hand knitting her way to the solution. Maigret, however, is a real policeman, not an inspired amateur. The criminals he deals every day are frequently inadequate, even pathetic. As head of the Paris criminal brigade, he has to manage his rather bland inspectors, Janvier, Lucas and LaPointe. They are all intelligent, loyal but rarely inspired. It is the criminals who are interesting. He also has to manage his superiors – the juges d'instruction. In the French system, these judges supervise the investigation of serious offences and are nervous of making political mistakes.

Though Simenon read Christie and Sayers, he was not remotely interested in the puzzle mystery. He made Maigret a subtle character, a detective with a solid marriage who is upset when he feels an investigation is not going well. Often he has sympathy with criminals. At times Maigret behaves like a confessor.

Another book is worth examining in detail. *Maigret Sets a Trap* begins as Paris is terrorised by a killer in the press compared to Jack the Ripper. Five women have been murdered, and the police have no leads. The killer knows the area where the murders have been committed very well. He knifes his victims in the street and then disappears.

At a dinner party Maigret meets Dr Tissot who runs St Anne's Hospital, one of the most famous asylums in Paris. After dinner, while their wives discuss recipes – Simenon obviously was no feminist – Maigret, Tissot and their host Dr Pardon settle over liqueurs to discuss theories of the killings. Tissot puts a series of questions to Maigret. Was there a pattern to the times when the murders were committed? Was there a pattern to the dates? Lightheartedly the men even touch on whether the killings took place when there was a full moon. Maigret tells his friends that the women were all of one physical type – slightly plump.

If he followed Freud and Adler blindly, Tissot says, he would conclude that killer was sexually obsessed, but none of the women were sexually assaulted. As a result, Tissot is sceptical. He guesses that the killer appears ordinary to those around him, a master masker of his true nature. Maigret feels frustrated because the inquiry makes no progress at all. It is then that he decides to set a trap.

Over liqueurs and theorising, Tissot suggests that many killers need to feel that they are important. They will hate the idea that someone else might get the credit for their crimes. So Maigret stages an arrest cleverly.

Simenon knew the workings of the press as well as psychiatry. Reporters wait in the corridors of the Police Judiciaire for anything. Then Maigret brings in a man who has a coat thrown over his head to hide his identity. Though he refuses to say anything the man must be a suspect, the reporters decide, which is just what Maigret wants. He gambles that, when the killer reads that another man has been arrested, he will strike again – and quickly to establish his claim to the murders.

The next night a number of policewomen walk through the streets as bait. One is attacked. Finally, Maigret has a clue because the policewoman decoy managed to pull a button off while struggling with her assailant. This button leads to a suit, and the suit leads to a young man who is effete, charming and outwardly utterly respectable, Moncin. Simenon makes Moncin almost a textbook case of psychoanalytic theories. His mother is possessive, so she arranged a marriage to a young woman she expected to be pliable. Mother was overconfident.

Moncin's wife Yvonne won the first battle between them as she got her husband to move out and take an apartment of their own. Her mother-in-law never forgave her. When Maigret accuses her beloved son of the murders she is furious. Yvonne is much calmer.

Moncin protests his innocence. Maigret shows his prisoner some sympathy, a weak man being fought over by a dominating mother and a sly wife. But Moncin will not confess. Then while Moncin is in custody, there is another murder. Comeliau, the investigating magistrate, is furious Maigret has taken the risk of setting a trap without telling him. The trap has gone badly wrong.

Stubbornly Moncin stays silent. Maigret now talks to Moncin more like a therapist than a policeman. He reassures him that he will not face the guillotine as it is obvious he is mad and suggests that might disappoint him as he can only escape the two women by dying. Then Maigret reconstructs the crimes and their background. His mother married a butcher and always felt she deserved better. In her flat, the police found many pictures of her beloved son but not one of her husband. The boy was delicate and brilliant, her only joy.

Moncin was never in love with his wife. He married to get some peace. He was not the star his mother hoped he would be, and his wife turned out not to be "a little turkey," but a woman who, in her own way, was as possessive as his mother. Both women stopped him being a real man, which Maigret thinks explains why Moncin did not sexually assault his victims. Maigret tells him he is sure he dreamed of killing both of them. He was smart enough to know that if he did that, he would be the prime suspect. He hated them, but he needed their protection which he found humiliating. He could not take his anger out on either of them, so he attacked women in general. He ripped their clothes, a symbolic act but rather a pathetic one.

A new murder while Moncin is in the cells infuriates the investigating magistrate who blames Maigret for getting it wrong. Maigret guesses though that either the mother or wife murdered to prove Moncin's innocence. He interrogates the two women, and a seemingly casual question is crucial. What was the colour of the dress the murderer woman wore? The mother flusters it was too dark to see, while the wife says calmly the dress was blue. She has won in fact. Maigret is so distressed he has to hold back tears and leaves one of his inspectors to charge her.

Finally, Maigret admits that no other case troubled him as much.

Simenon also wrote a semi-autobiographical novel that revealed some of his own insecurities.

Letter to a Judge

The author of the book is being tried for murder, and he addresses his letter to Comineau, the judge Maigret has to report to. The author admits that during five weeks of almost daily interrogation what the judge thought of him mattered and he was sure that he was an interesting case. He flatters himself that Comineau, the judge, tried to understand him not just for professional reasons but as a man. The book snipes at the local press Simenon started in as the papers report on "the hideous smile of the accused." A phrase Simenon may well have used as a young reporter.

The rest of the book appears an autobiography, but Simenon ends with a paradox. He decided to murder his wife Martine though he loves her dearly and, in fact, because he loves her dearly. He was always sharp on the paradoxes of love. He describes her death as the only way out for him.

Simenon told the doctors he feared ending up like Nietzsche whose brilliant career ended when he was committed to any asylum at the age of 44. But they countered this was just an alibi because Nietzsche suffered from organic brain disease – and Simenon showed no sign of that. His own career ended with his being accepted as one of France's greatest 20th-century writers. One of the rewards of writing this book has been reading and re-reading his work. His reputation has only increased after his death.

Chapter 12

Curtains

Contemporary psychology, pathology porn and the enduring link with detective fiction

In June 2020, during the Coronavirus crisis, sales of crime novels boomed. *The Guardian* reported that 120,000 more were sold that month than in June 2019. To cope with stress what better than a good whodunnit?

In the classic detective novel, the finale is routine. We find out who is guilty and how they "dunnit." The genre, however, has developed in the past 20 years and, often, the science invoked is genetics rather than psychology.

I have stressed the similarities between the work of the detective and that of the analyst, but there is one difference. The analyst does not usually end with a cheery, "I have found all your complexes, explained them to you so get off the couch. You have been cured, you will have no more problems." The detective story provides a true "the end." Wimsey or Poirot invites all those involved to listen as they explain what really happened.

I have tried throughout the book to summarise key psychological "moments" as they affect crime fiction, but psychology has changed. In my first book *Psychologists on Psychology,* I interviewed 13 of the world's great psychologists. Many of them like Skinner had grand theories of human behaviour as Freud had. One of the most endearing Niko Tinbergen, who won a Nobel, was an animal behaviour specialist, but he also used his findings to offer a comprehensive theory of autism. Psychology has become far more specialised, and it is almost impossible for one person to master its whole range. As a result, there are fewer grand theories of human behaviour. Psychology has nevertheless arrived at some conclusions about what makes someone a killer or a serial killer.

DOI: 10.4324/9780429344664-12

The history and profile of serial killers

In the 15th century, a former companion-in-arms, Gilles De Rais sexually assaulted and killed peasant children, mainly boys he had abducted from the surrounding villages. Estimates of those he slaughtered range from 140 and 800.

The most prolific female serial killer was Elisabeth Bathory, a 17th-century Hungarian countess who terrorised her servants. After her husband died – she probably killed him – she became maniacally violent. She and four collaborators were accused of torturing and killing hundreds of girls and young women. Being an aristocrat Elizabeth was not tried but just imprisoned in Csejte Castle. The killings stopped once she was behind its walls.

In 1886, Richard Krafft Ebbing in *Psychopathia Sexualis* examined the case of a serial murderer in the 1870s, Eusebius Pieydagnelle, who had a sexual obsession with blood and confessed to murdering six people.

The psychology of serial killers has prompted many studies, but they tend to stress one factor which echoes Bowlby's work – childhood problems.

When Jack the Ripper murdered five prostitutes in the 1880s, the police surgeon Thomas Bond was asked to give his opinion on the extent of the murderer's surgical skill and knowledge. In notes, dated 10 November 1888, Bond highlighted the sexual nature of the murders. He concluded that

> the murderer must have been a man of physical strength and great coolness and daring ... subject to periodic attacks of homicidal and erotic mania. The characters of the mutilations indicate that the man may be in a condition sexually, that may be called Satyriasis.

The profile did not help catch the killer.

Jack the Ripper and Krafft Ebbing's 1886 cases were the first of many, some of which made profilers famous. In 1956, the psychiatrist Dr James Brussel hit the headlines after his profile of New York City's "mad bomber" was published in the *New York Times*. The media dubbed him "The Sherlock Holmes of the Couch." In his 1968 book *Casebook of a Crime Psychiatrist*, Brussel claimed he predicted that the bomber would wear a buttoned-up double-breasted suit but edited out the many incorrect predictions he had also made. He boasted, for example, that he had successfully pre-dicted the bomber would be a Slav who lived in Connecticut when he had actually predicted the killer would be "born and educated in Germany," and live in White Plains, New York.

Such inflated claims helped make the FBI director J. Edgar Hoover sceptical about profiling. It was only after his death in 1972 that the FBI Behavioural Science Unit was formed – the unit which featured in the 1990 hit film *The Silence of the Lambs* and others.

The influence of behaviourism on the Unit is clear. Two senior FBI agents, John Douglas and Robert Ressler, created the Unit. They interviewed serial predators in jail to get obtain information about their motives, planning and preparation, details of the crimes, and how they disposed of evidence, especially the bodies of victims. Their aim was to compile a central database in which the motives of serial offenders were matched with crime scene information. They got a $1 million research grant to design a computerised database system called the Violent Criminal Apprehension Program (VICAP). This allowed the FBI to cross-reference information from open cases involving serial predators to closed cases in order to match beha-vioural characteristics and patterns. A key premise was that the personality of an unknown perpetrator could be predicted "as be-haviour reflects personality," said retired FBI special agent Gregg McCrary.

The logic was common sense, and an example of the association of ideas Hume would have approved. An example, "if the victim was found at the scene of the crime with no apparent attempt to conceal the body, then the offender is likely to be a spontaneous killer who does not meticulously plan a murder prior to committing it."

Every time the research team learned something new about the behaviour of serial offenders the information was programmed into Profiler. Profiler is a tool, not a substitute for human analysis.

In a serial homicide case, according to McCrary, as reported by the APA's *Monitor on Psychology* in 2004, FBI agents get insights into criminal personality by answering questions about the mur-derer's behaviour at four different crime phases. I have put in italics those that involve behaviour.

- Antecedent: What fantasy or plan, or perhaps both, did the murderer have in place before committing the act of murder? *What triggered the murderer to act sometimes and not others?*

- Method and manner: *What type of victim or victims did the murderer select? What was the method and manner of murder – that is, shooting, stabbing, strangulation, poisoning or something else?*
- Body disposal: *Did the murder and body disposal take place all at one scene or multiple scenes? Was there an attempt to hide the bodies?*
- Post-offence behaviour: Is the murderer trying to inject himself/ herself into the investigation by reacting to news media reports or contacting police investigators? This is partly a matter of behaviour (Winerman 2004).

In my ITV film about the Soham murders *When Holly Went Missing*, it became clear that the police began to suspect Ian Huntley of killing Holly Wells and Jessica Chapman, partly because of the way he kept coming forward to them with information.

By 1996, 12 FBI profilers were applying profiling to approximately 1,000 cases per year. In the United Kingdom, 29 profilers provided 242 instances of profiling advice between 1981 and 1994. Sweden, Finland, Russia, Canada, the Netherlands and New Zealand also used it. The appeal of profiling is logical. Its five basic steps include analysing the crime and comparing it to similar crimes in the past; an in-depth analysis of the crime scene; considering the victim's background and activities for possible motives and connections; considering other possible motives and developing a description of the possible offender that can be compared with previous cases. Surveys of police officers in the United States, the United Kingdom and Canada have found that an overwhelming majority consider profiling to be useful.

The FBI Unit is central to *The Silence of the Lambs*, a novel that became a brilliant film. Thomas Harris made his psychoanalyst "hero" a killer and gives a full background for Hannibal Lecter. He was born into old Baltic nobility, on 20 January 1933. During the war, his family fled their castle, but his parents were killed, leaving Hannibal and Mischa, his little sister, to fend for themselves. They took refuge in a chalet which was attacked by soldiers who were starving. They killed Mischa and devour her body. An extraordinary predator was born as a result of seeing his sister killed and eaten.

Hannibal returns to the family castle, converted into an orphanage after the war. On his 13th birthday, he flees and goes to his aunt's house. There he commits his first murder by killing Paul Momund, a butcher and war criminal. Hannibal thus avenges an insult to the Japanese wife of his uncle, Dame Murasaki. Bowlby would not have been surprised Hannibal became a killer.

Then Hannibal leaves for Paris with Dame Murasaki. He studies medicine, tracks down his sister's murderers and tastes his revenge. They ate his sister, so he will eat them. He develops a taste for cannibalism and for a first-class claret to accompany it.

Hannibal emigrates to America, where he becomes a respected psychiatrist and a member of the committee of the Baltimore Philharmonic Orchestra. Being a poor musician seems to be risky in detective fiction. In one book of Gladys Mitchell, a musician pays the ultimate price for an imperfect performance. The Baltimore orchestra too has one weak player – the flautist Benjamin Raspail who is killed so no one will have to listen to him play poorly again.

Hannibal then serves the committee a strange stew "whose ingredients were never identified" (the flautist was also one of the "amuse-bouches"), accompanied naturally by a fine wine. Before being caught Hannibal massacres eight people in all.

Surveys of police officers in the United States, the United Kingdom and Canada have found that an overwhelming majority consider profiling to be useful. The research does not support this, however.

Pinizzotto and Finkel (1990) showed that trained profilers did not do anything better than non-profilers in producing an accurate profile of the criminal. A 2000 study also showed that profilers were not significantly better at creating a profile than any other group that had access to all the details of a crime.

A 2007 meta-analysis of research noted that there was "a notable incongruity between [profiling's] lack of empirical foundation and the degree of support for the field." Malcolm Gladwell of the *New Yorker* compared profiling to astrology. Other critics like Brent Snook sniped it was an investigative tool that was not backed up by consistent scientific evidence. In *The Silence of the Lambs,* Hannibal has the great advantage of having analysed one of the killers. Scientific doubts about profiling have not stopped fiction writers from detailing cases where profilers have helped solve murders.

Wilson and Seaman (1990) concluded that the most influential factor that contributed to their homicidal activity was they had experienced some sort of problems during their childhood. Their parents split or failed to provide a structured disciplined home or abused them. Nearly half of the serial killers in the 1990 study had experienced some type of physical or sexual abuse, and more of them had experienced emotional neglect. Freud would not have been surprised at all, but there is an as-yet unanswered question which psychiatrists have not resolved. Most children who experience abuse do not become abusers, let alone killers, let alone serial killers. The novel that tells the story of a child who survives abuse but does not take revenge on others will be a novelty.

In the beginning, I noted that 63% of American undergraduates had "homicidal ideation." In 2019, 2,345 murderers in the United States were aged 20 and 24. Young killers but still a tiny fraction of the 19 million people of that age in the United States. Official figures also make the fantastic claim there were four murderers between the ages of one and four.

One of the most unsavoury and bizarre aspects of the "popularity" of serial killers is the market that has developed in their memorabilia. The killers' paintings, writings and poems all command high prices. Recently, this commercial obscenity has got worse. You can buy trading cards and action figures of the most brutal murderers. As far as I know, there are no Poirot or Wimsey or Miss Marple dolls on the market.

Readers who want to make sure they have not missed a thing can consult *The Serial Killer Files: The Who, What, Where, How, and Why of the World's Most Terrifying Murderers* and *The A-Z Encyclopaedia of Serial Killers* by Schecter and David Everitt.

Genetics

Dr Watson, admittedly not the most up-to-date medic in his time, had not much of a clue about genetics even though Mendel's experiments on breeding different kinds of peas were well known by the 1890s. Today detective novels often involve DNA and tracing any guilty person careless enough to leave a stray hair at the scene.

In 1986, I filmed Alex Jeffreys of Leicester University who did much of the early research on DNA fingerprinting for a Channel 4 film about immigration. The Home Office believed many people applying to enter Britain from the Indian subcontinent were lying about being related to someone who was already living in the United Kingdom. I was allowed to film two senior immigration officers as they trekked to villages in India and Bangladesh to test people who made such claims. They often felt baffled by who was who, but they battled on. Once they confessed (under an umbrella in the heat but they were civil servants rarely parted from their brollies) how confusing it all was. Not cricket at all.

The Home Office was sure most of the claims would be false. But when Jeffreys compared the DNA of the would-be immigrants with those of their alleged relatives in the United Kingdom, he found many positive matches. The Home Office could not ignore the science. Jeffreys was knighted properly for his work. Fiction now often has DNA fingerprinting as a major clue.

It is also worth examining the growing popularity of detective fiction.

The thriller goes global

The detective story was never the preserve of Anglo Saxons even in the 1890s. Now it is less so than ever. A quick overview of its spread is fun. Brazil is a country where psychoanalysis and psychotherapy have flourished, and its detective fiction reflects that with works like *O Matador*. Nordic noir has become a genre all of its own. Wallander is the most famous of the Nordic detectives, but for me, the most engaging detail about sleuthing in Norway is its so-called reindeer detectives. It would be nice to imagine they investigate four-footed delinquents who steal the flashiest toys from Santa's gift bag, but they're just ordinary policemen and women who sometimes use reindeer to solve crimes beyond the Arctic Circle.

Icelandic fiction and fact also intertwine. A key character is Gisli Gudjuddson who began his career as a detective in Iceland and then became a psychologist. He was MacKeith's colleague in their pioneering work on false confessions. Iceland in reality has had some peculiar unsolved crimes where unreliable confessions have led to unsafe convictions. There are also many fictions set in Iceland including the Inspector Erlender mysteries.

Travelling further north I had not expected to find crime fiction in Greenland whose total population in 2018 was 56,025 but at least 28 detective tales are set there. They cover familiar themes as the motives for murder include fear, greed and jealousy. Incidentally, if Edgar Allen Poe made an ourang-outang the killer in the *Rue Morgue*, why can't we have a psychopathic whale, ideally a sea monster descended from the fish that swallowed

Jonah. Pierre Bayard would enjoy filleting the psychology of such an adventure.

Russia, China, India, even Outer Mongolia all have their gumshoes too, and they often rely on psychological insights to hunt killers. Only Antarctica seems sleuth-free ... so far.

The decline of the puzzle

The genre has changed. Most evidently the puzzle element has become less central than in the 1920s and 1930s, so that it is not the main element and, in some cases, not any part of the story at all. There are unsolved crimes where the puzzle (far too frivolous a word for real unsolved crimes) remains. The identity of Jack the Ripper has generated over 100 books – none of which are conclusive. Every police force has files on so-called cold cases, some of which are becoming less cold as long as the police can garner some DNA evidence.

The decline of the puzzle element is illustrated in the rise of the police procedural. Val McDermid's *Still Life* is an excellent example of both the police procedural and how far we have moved from the killings in a thatched cottage country village. As the Scottish police pursue suspects McDermid covers the procedure in Scotland, Eire, France, Northern Ireland and Holland. The book details different procedures in different countries. One suspect is even subject to a European Arrest warrant which has to be obtained in four hours. The book also offers the details of the procedures of autopsy ancient and modern – a development that has become popular in the last 20 years.

Fact supports fiction. In an excellent memoir *In the Office of Constable*, written by Robert Mark who was Commissioner of the Metropolitan Police from 1972 to 1977, a period that included the Guildford murders. Mark reported many cases whose solution he had supervised. Many were brutal killings, but there was hardly one in which there was a puzzle or any doubt as to who was guilty. Mark's two most famous "cases" were political. In the Spaghetti House Siege, some robbers were trapped in the Knightsbridge restaurant they had been robbing. They claimed to have been victims of racism and eventually surrendered. Mark's other triumph was the Balcombe Street siege where four IRA men took refuge after an operation that went wrong. They held two hostages for six days in December 1976. The police negotiators were deft, and the siege ended without any deaths.

In neither of these cases was there a question as to who did it. The police procedural fascinates, however, because it takes the reader behind the scenes. It is not the workings of Poirot's little grey cells that intrigues but how a large organisation works in its efforts to get the guilty.

Another development has been the study of body language which began in the 1970s with the work of the social psychologist Michael Argyle. Police training now involves teaching body language. Its basic idea is that "tells" give clues to what someone thinks and feels; they are unconscious reactions as the body leaks its truths. Fidgeting and avoiding eye contact are strong hints as to areas detectives should probe. A number of textbooks list such "tells" in detail, though from early on body language researchers realised some men and women were "Machiavellian"; these individuals could lie while looking you straight and sincerely in the eyes. Again fiction now often involves the detectives analysing body language. How reliable such evidence is dubious, however.

Pathology porn

The detective novel also meets science in so-called pathology porn. Edmund Wilson in 1946 argued the detective novel was so popular because it pinpointed the guilty and helped ward off our anxieties about death. Today our anxieties demand more detail. The many successful novels about pathology – and the long-running BBC series *Silent Witness* – show that every grisly detail about the decay of the body and the putrefaction we all come to is as good box office as Christie and Sayers were in their day. The grandes dames of the genre Patricia Cornwell and Kathy Reichs are also pathologists in real life, which gives their work great authority. They give riveting accounts of how bones and tissues yield the truth. Three of Reich's titles include the word Bones, just to make sure readers know they will get the blood, gore and forensics they expect.

Writers now tell us more about their detectives too. Poirot and Miss Marple were one-dimensional, though Peter Wimsey was not, and even changed in the course of his career, mastering his depression and ending up happily married. Some other writers have also fleshed their detectives out. P.D. James' Adam Dalgleish is far too intellectual to grow one vegetable marrow and the idea that he might enter his prize exhibit in the Kings Langley concours de courgettes is utterly impossible. Dalgleish writes poetry instead. He is also a widower who still hankers after true love which he finally finds. Though Poirot has fantasies about a seductive duchess he nearly tangled with he never comes close to even kissing her. His true love is Captain Hastings one suspects.

We know virtually nothing of Miss Marple's lost love beyond the fact that he died in the 1914 war.

Ian Rankin has written some 20 books where John Rebus is the detective. Rankin makes Rebus a complex personality – he drinks too much, seems to think police procedure is a curse and drives his assistant Siobhan to distraction though she adores him. They never sleep together though. Rebus solves crimes partly by routine police work, partly by intuition and partly because he has such close links to Edinburgh's top criminal Big Ger. A recent story claimed a man posing as Big Ger posted material on Rankin's Facebook page; it was soon taken down.

The classic detective novel has metamorphosed into something more lurid, but which still reflects our need to imagine and reflect on violence and death. It seems likely the interplay between psychology psychiatry and detective fiction will continue.

In 2036, it will be 150 years since the first Holmes story and the start of Freud's work on the unconscious mind. It is of course an accident that both happened the same year.

Or is it?

Someone should start planning the 2036 celebrations.

References

Adler, A. (2013) *The Science of Living* (Psychology Revivals) Routledge London

Adler, A. (2013) *Understanding Human Nature* (Psychology Revivals) Routledge London

Ainsworth, M. (1967) *Infancy in Uganda; Infant Care and the Growth of Love* Johns Hopkins Press Baltimore

Ainsworth, M. D. S., Blehar, M. C., Waters, E., & Wall, S. (1978) *Patterns of Attachment: A Psychological Study of the Strange Situation.* Psychology Press London

Alfred, Hitchcock (1941) *Suspicion*, a film starring Cary Grant

Anticipatory Plagiarism New literary history a journal of theory and interpretation. VOL 44; NUMB 2; 2013, 231-250 – The Johns Hopkins University Press Part 2; (pages 231–250) – 2013n

Aristotle (1957) (c.350) *On the Soul. Parva Naturalia. On Breath.* translated by W.S. Hett Loeb Classical Library 288. Harvard University Press Cambridge, MA

Aristotle (1987) (c.350) *De Anima* Penguin Classics

Aries, Philippe (1996) *Centuries of Childhood* Pimlico London

Axelrod, George (1965) *How to Murder Your Wife* (Dir, Richard Quine,) Murder Inc. United Artists

Bayard, Pierre (2007) translated by Mehlman, Jeffrey *How to Talk about Books You Haven't Read* Bloomsbury London

Berger, Arthur Asa (2003) *Durkheim Is Dead! Sherlock Holmes Is Introduced to Social Theory* Alta Mira Press Lanham, Maryland USA

Berkeley, George (1709) *An Essay Towards a New Theory of Vision* printed by Aaron Rhames, for Jeremy Pepyat

Berkeley, Anthony (pseudonym Francis Ilse) (1926) *The Wychofrd Poisoning Case* 1926 US edition published by Doubleday, The Crime Club Inc 1930

Berkeley, Anthony (pseudonym Francis Ilse) (1929) *The Poisoned Chocolate Case* William Collins, Sons London

Berkeley, Anthony (pseudonym Francis Ilse) (1939) *As for the Woman* Jarrolds London

Berkeley, Anthony (pseudonym Francis Ilse) (1940) *O England* Hamish Hamilton London

Berkeley, Anthony (pseudonym Francis Ilse) (2010) *The Layton Court Mystery* published anonymously 1925 and by Langtail Press

Berkeley, Anthony (pseudonym Francis Ilse) (2011) *Before the Fact* Arcturus Publishing Ltd London

Boeree, C. G. (2006) *Personality Theories: Hans Eysenck and Others* Scientific Research Publishing London

Bonaparte, Princess Marie (1933) *The Life and Works of Edgar Allan Poe. A Psycho-Analytic Interpretation* (first published in French in 1933) and Imago publishing company (1949)

Bond, Henry (2012) *Lacan at the Scene* MIT Press Cambridge Mass

Bronte, Charlotte (1847) *Jane Eyre* Smith, Elder and Co. London

Brooks, Frederick (1975) *Mythical Man-Month: Essays on Software Engineering* Addison-Wesley and (1995) Addison-Wesley Professional Boston

Brussel, James (1970) *A Casebook of a Crime Psychiatrist* Mayflower Paperbacks, London

Charcot, J-M. (1888) *Nouvelle Iconographie de Salpêtrière. Clinique des maladies du systeme nerveux. Publiée sous la direction du par Paul Richer, Gilles de la Tourette, Albert Londe.* Lecrosnier et Babé Paris

Chaucer, G (2005) *(1476) The Canterbury Tales* William Caxton and Penguin Classics Harmondsworth

Chesterton, G. K. (1911) *The Innocence of Father Brown* Cassell and Company London.

Christie, Agatha (1920) *The Mysterious Affair at Styles* Penguin Books 1935 and 2013 Harper Collins London

Christie, Agatha (1960) *Four-and-Twenty Blackbirds* published in *The Adventure of the Christmas Pudding and a Selection of Entrées* Collins Crime Club London

Christie, Agatha (1961) *The Pale Horse* and (2017) Harper Collins London

Christie, Agatha (1964) *A Caribbean Holiday* Collins Crime Club London

Christie, Agatha (1972) *Elephants Can Remember* Collins Crime Club London

Christie, Agatha (1975) *Curtain: Poirott's Last Case* Collins Crime Club London

Christie, Agatha (1976) *The Sleeping Murder* Collins Crime Club London

Christie, Agatha (1977) *Psychologists on Psychology* Routledge London

Christie, Agatha (2003) *Nemesis* Harper Collins London

Christie, Agatha (2008) *Ordeal by Innocence* Harper Collins London

Christie, Agatha (2010) *An Autobiography* Harper Collins London

Christie, Agatha (2010) *Murder on the Orient Express* Harper Collins London

Christie, Agatha (2010) *Death on the Nile* Harper Collins London

Christie, Agatha (2011) *The Sleeping Murder* Harper Collins London

Christie, Agatha (2013) *And Then There Were None* Harper Collins London

Christie, Agatha (2013) *The ABC Murders* Harper Collins London

Christie, Agatha (2013) *The Murder of Roger Ackroyd* Harper Collins London

Christie, Agatha (2015) *And Then There Were None* Harper Collins London

Christie, Agatha (2015) *Death in the Clouds* Harper Collins London

Christie, Agatha (2017) *Murder on the Orient Express* Harper Collins London

Christie, Agatha (2017) *Black Coffee* Harper Collins London

Christie, Agatha (2017) *The Postern of Fate* Harper Collins London

Christie, Agatha (2018) *Cards on the Table* Harper Collins London

Christie, Agatha (2019) *Murder She Said: The Quotable Miss Marple* Harper Collins Publishers London

Churchill, Winston (1946) *The Dream Unpublished MS* in The Churchill Archives Cambridge

Cobb, Matthew (2020) *The Idea of the Brain* Profile London

Cohen, D. (1985) *The Development of Laughter* PhD thesis University of London

Cohen, D. (2012) *Freud on Coke* Cutting Edge Press London

Collins, Wilkie (1859) *The Woman in White* published in Charles Dickens' magazine *All the Year Round* also Penguin Classics 2003 Harmondsworth

Collins, Wilkie (1868) *The Moonstone* William Tinsley London

Collins, Wilkie (1875) *The Law and the Lady* Chatto & Windus London

Conan Doyle, Arthur (1879) *Gelseminum as a poison. British Medical Journal* 2, 483

Conan Doyle, Arthur (1887) *A Study in Scarlet* Ward Lock and Co. London

Conan Doyle, Arthur (1890) *The Surgeon of Gaster Fell* in *Chamber's Journal* December 1890 Vol. 7, 6 pp. 770–773, December 13, 1890, pp. 787–790, December 20, 1890, pp. 802–805, December 27, 1890, pp. 819–822

Conan Doyle, Arthur (1891) *A Scandal in Bohemia* article published in *The Strand Magazines* Vol. 7 July 1891

Conan Doyle, Arthur (1903) *The Adventure of the Empty House* in *The Strand Magazine* Vol. 10

Conan Doyle, Arthur (1902) *The Hound of the Baskervilles* in *The Strand Magazine* Vol. 22 and 23

Conan Doyle, Arthur (1920) *Fairies Photographed: An Epoch-Making Event Described by A. Conan Doyle* article published in *The Strand Magazine* December 1920

Cournos, John (1932) *The Devil Is an English Gentleman 1932* and Kessinger Publishing (2005)

Dante's *The Divine Comedy* translation Dorothy Sayers three vols issued between 1949 and 1962 Penguin Classics Harmondsworth

Darwin, Charles (1872) *The Expression of Emotions in Animals and Men* John Murray, London

Delafield, E. M. (1929) *The Messalina of the Suburbs* Macmillan and Co. London

Doolittle, Hilda (1984) *A Tribute to Freud* New Directions Publishing, New York

Eco, Umberto (1980) *The Name of the Rose Bompiani, Italy* Harcourt Boston USA

Eliot, T.S. (1935) *Murder in the Cathedral* Faber and Faber London

Faye, Lindsay (2017) *Jane Steele* G.P. Putnam's Sons New York

Fichtl, Paula (1999) *La Famille Freud au jour le jour* PUF Paris

Fielding, Henry (1749) *A History of Tom Jones* Andrew Millar and Penguin Classics Harmondsworth

Fowlers, Orson (1839) *American Phrenological Journal and Miscellany* Philadelphia New York, 58–64.

Freud, S. (1895) *Project for a Scientific Psychology* The Standard Edition of the Complete Psychological Works of Sigmund Freud, Vol. I (1950)

Freud, S. (1901)*The Psychopathology of Everyday Life* and standard Edition Penguin London 2002

Freud, S. (1903) *Jokes and The Relation to the Unconscious* and Standard edition Random House London Vol. 8 2001

Freud, S. (1913) *Totem and Taboo* Standard Edition Vintage Publishing London Vol. 13. 2001

Freud, S. (1914) *History of the Psychoanalytic Movement* and Standard edition Random House London Vol. 14. 2001

Freud, S. (1995) *The standard edition of the complete psychological works of Sigmund Freud* translated from the German under the general editorship of James Strachey; in collaboration with Anna Freud; assisted by Alix Strachey and Alan Tyson; editorial assistant, Angela Richards. Hogarth Press and the Institute of Psycho-analysis: London

Gauld, Alan (1992) *A History of Hypnosis* Cambridge University Press Cambridge

Gibb, Andrew ("Captain X") (1924) *With Winston Churchill at the Front* Cowens & Gray, Ltd. London

Gilles de la Tourette, G. (1895) *Traité Clinique et Thérapeutique de L'hystérie, D'après L'enseignement de la Salpetriere. I. Hystérie*

Normale ou Interparoxystique; II-III. Hystérie Paroxystique. Plon et Nourrit Paris

Glendinning, Victoria (1995) *Electricity: A Novel* Little Brown and co. New York

Goldstein, R. L. (1986) *Forensic psychiatry and literature: I. Simenon's Syndrome or De Clérambault's Syndrome? A psycho-literary postscript to erotomania. Psychiatric Journal of the University of Ottawa,* 11(1), 15–17.

Gordon, H. (2012) *Broadmoor* Psychology News Press London

Gramsci, A. (1985) *The Detective Novel* in *Selections from Cultural Writings* Lawrence and Wishart London

Gurney, Edmund, Myers, F. W. H., & Podmore, Frank (1886) *Phantasms of the Living.* 2 vols. Society for Psychical Research, Trubner & Co. London.

Hamilton Fyfe, W. (1940) *Aristotle's Art of Poetry* Clarendon Press Oxford

Hartley, David (1749) *Observations on Man, His Frame, His Duty, and His Expectations* Samuel Richardson London

Hartley, David (1999) *David Hartley on Human Nature* University Press of New York, New York

Harris, Thomas (1980) *The Silence of the Lambs* St. Martin's New York

Hartman, Donald K. (2018) *Death by Suggestion: An Anthology of 19th and Early 20th-Century Tales of Hypnotically Induced Murder, Suicide, and Accidental Death* Create Space Independent Publishing Platform

Heretics (1905) Dover publications (2006) London

Hoffman, Edward (1994) *The Drive for Self: Alfred Adler and the Founding of Individual Psychology* Addison-Wesley New York

Homer (1965) *The Iliad* Penguin Classics Harmondsworth

Hull, Clark H. (1933) *Hypnosis and Suggestibility: An Experimental Approach* Crown House Publishing Carmarthen, Wales. 2002.

Hume, David (1896) *A Treatise of Human Nature by David Hume, reprinted from the Original Edition in three volumes and edited, with an analytical index,* by L.A. Selby-Bigge, Clarendon Press and (1985) Penguin Classics: M.A. Oxford

Huston, Johndir. (1963) *Freud the Secret Passion* produced by Bavaria Film at Universal Studios, Hollywood.

Ibsen, Henrik (1972) *Peer Gynt* Offcut Private Press Leicester.

Ing, Robert (2010) "The Art of Forensic Detection and Sherlock Holmes," published at http://www.drroberting.com/articles/holmes.pdf

James, William (1902) *The Varieties of Religious Experience: A Study in Human Nature,* Longmans, Green and Co. New York, based on the *Gifford Lectures on Natural Religion* delivered at the University of Edinburgh in 1901 and 1902.

James, William (1985) *Psychology: Briefer Course (The Works of William James)* Harvard University Press Harvard

Jones, Ernest (1931) *The Elements of Figure Skating* Methuen and Co London

Jones, Ernest (1974) *The Life and Work of Sigmund* Freud Basic Books

Jones, Ernest (1976) *The Life and Work of Sigmund* Freud Basic Books New York

Keating, Peter (2017) *Agatha Christie and Shrewd Miss Marple* Priskus Books London

Koffka, Kurt (1924) *Growth of the Mind: An Introduction to Child Psychology* Liveright Publishing New York

Koffka, Kurt (1925) *The Growth of the Mind: An Introduction to Child-psychology.* (R. M. Ogden, Trans.) International Library of Psychology, Philosophy and Scientific Method. Kegan Paul Trench & Trubner London

Koffka, Kurt (1935) *Principles of Gestalt Psychology* Mimesis International, 2014.

Krafft-Ebing, Richard von (1886) *Psychopathis Sexualis* 1886 and Arcade publishing 2011

Krajbich, Ian & Konovalov, Arkady (2018) *Neurocomputational Dynamics of Sequence Learning* in Neuron, 2018 DOI: 10.1016/j.neuron.2018.05.013

Lacan, Jacques (1973) Les quatre concepts fondamentaux de la psychanalyse, *The Seminar of Jacques Lacan: The Four Fundamental Concepts of Psychoanalysis* 1998 W. W. Norton Company London

Le Carre, John (1962) *A Murder of Quality* Gollancz London

Leri, Andre (1919) *Shell Shock: Commotional and Emotional Aspects* University of London Press London

Locke, John (2004) *An Essay Concerning Human Understanding* Wordsworth London

Lustgarten, Edgar (1949) *Verdict in Dispute* Allan Wingate London and New York

Mark, Robert (1979) *In the Office of Constable* Fontana Paperbacks London

Masterman, Charles Frederick Gurney (1909) *The Condition of England* Methuen London

Maslanka, Chris (2020) *Two Thousand Years of Puzzling* Radio 4

McDermid, Val (2020) *Still Life* Little Brown London

Meyer, Nicholas (1974) *The 7 Percent Solution* E P Dutton New York

Mitchell, Gladys (1929) *Speedy Death* Victor Gollancz and Vintage Press London 2014

Mitchell, Gladys (1929) *The Mystery of a Butcher's Shop* Victor Gollancz London

Mitchell, Gladys (1932) *The Saltmarsh Murders* Victor Gollancz London

Mitchell, Gladys (1944) *The Winnowing – 44 Poems* Wright and Sons London

Myers, Charles S. (1916) *Contributions to the Study of Shell Shock. Being an Account of Certain Cases Treated with Hypnosis* in The Lancet, January 8, 1916, 65–69

Nasruddin, Mullah (1968) *The Pleasantries of the Incredible Mulla Nasrudin* Octagon Press and 1993 Penguin Harmondsworth

Ohio State University. (2018) *"This is your brain detecting patterns: It is different from other kinds of learning, study shows."* ScienceDaily, 31 May

Orwell (1939) *Coming Up for Air* Victor Gollancz London

Orwell (1965) *The Decline of the English Murder* Penguin Harmondsworth

Owen, Wilfred (1931) *Anthem for Doomed Youth* in *The Poems of Wilfred Owen* Chatto and Windus London.

Packard, Vance (1960) *The Hidden Persuaders* Penguin Harmondsworth

Philipps, Adam (2014) *Becoming Freud* Yale University Press New Haven

Pinizzotto, A. J. & Finkel, N. J. (1990) *Criminal personality profiling: An outcome and process study. Law and Human Behavior*, 14(3), 215–233

Poe, Edgar Allan (1841) *The Murders in the Rue Morgue* in *Graham's Magazine* Volume XVIII, Number 4

Polidori, J. (1819) *The Vampire* Sherwood, Neely, and Jones London

Redmond, Christopher (1984) *In Bed with Sherlock Holmes: Sexual Elements in Arthur Conan Doyle's Stories of the Great Detective* Dundurn Toronto

Reid, Fiona (2010) *Broken Men: Shell Shock, Treatment and Recovery in Britain 1914-1930* Continuum London and New York

Read, Herbert (1946) *To a Conscript of 1940* in *Collected Poems* Faber and Faber London

Reynolds, J. & McCrea, S. (2017) *Spontaneous Violence and Homicide Thoughts in Four Homicide Contexts Psychiat. Psychology Law*, 24, 605–27

Richet, Charles & Joseph, Maxwell (1905) *Metapsychical Phenomena: Methods and Observations* Duckworth London

Rivers, W. H. R. (1917) *An Address on the Repression of War Experience*, delivered before the Section of Psychiatry, Royal Society of Medicine, December 4

Rivers, W. H. R. (1889) *Delirium and Its Allied Conditions* read before the Abernethian Society (*St. Bart's Hospital Reports*, 25, pp. 279–280)

Rivers, W. H. R. (1891) *Hysteria* read before the Abernethian Society (*St. Bart's Hospital Reports*, 27, pp. 285–286)

Rivers, W. H. R. (1893) *Neurasthenia* read before the Abernethian Society (*St. Bart's Hospital Reports*, 29, p. 350)

Rivers, W. H. R. (1923) *Conflict and Dreams* (1999) Psychology Press Hove

Rhys, Jean (1966) *The Wide Sargasso Sea* André Deutsch London

Sartre, Jean Paul (1943) *Being and Nothingness* Éditions Gallimard Paris

Sartre, Jean Paul (1943) *Les Mouches* Gallimard Paris

Sartre, Jean Paul (1947) *Huis Clos* Gallimard Paris

Sartre, Jean Paul (1948) *Les Mains Sales* Gallimard Paris

Sayers. (1923) *Who's Body?* T Fisher Unwin London

Sayers. (1928) *The Fascinating Problem of Uncle Meleager* in *Lord Peter Views the Body* Victor Gollancz Ltd London

Sayers. (1930) *The Documents in the Case* Ernest Benn London

Sayers. (1932) *Have His Carcase* Victor Gollancz London

Sayers. (1933) *Murder Must Advertise* Victor Gollancz London

Sayers. (1935) *Gaudy Night* Victor Gollancz Ltd London

Sayers. (1936) *How I came to invent the character of Lord Peter Wimsey* in *Harcourt Brace News*, July 15th 1936

Sayers. (1939) *The Devil to Pay* Victor Gollancz London

Sayers. (1941) *The Mind of the Maker* Methuen & Co. Ltd. London

Sayers. (1943) *The Man Born to Be King* Victor Gollancz London

Sayers. (1946) Dorothy

Sayers. (1946) *Unpopular Opinions* Victor Gollancz London

Schechter. (2003) Harold and Everett, David *The Serial Killer Files: The Who, What, Where, How, and Why of the World's Most Terrifying Murderers* Ballatine Books New York

Schechter. (2006) *The A-Z Encyclopaedia of Serial Killers* Simon and Schuster New York and London

Sherlock Holmes was Wrong: Re-opening the Case of the "Hound of the Baskervilles" (2007) translated by Charlotte Mandell Bloomsbury USA *Who Killed Roger Ackroyd* (2001) (co authored with Carol Cosman) William Collins, Sons London, New York

Simenon, Georges (1944) *Monsieur Lundi* Gallimard Paris

Simenon, Georges (1947) *Lettre à mon juge* (Letter to My Judge) Presses de la Cité Paris

Simenon, Georges (1952) *Le Revolver de Maigret* and *Maigret's Revolver: Inspector Maigret* and 1956 Hamish Hamilton (UK) 1984 Harcourt (US) Penguin Classics (2017)

Simenon, Georges (1955) *Maigret sets a trap* Presses de la Cité Paris

Simenon, Georges (1970) *La Folle de Maigret* Presses de la Cité Paris

Shakespeare, William (2015) Hamlet Penguin Classics

Shakespeare, William (2015) Macbeth Penguin Classics

Shakespeare, William (2015) Richard III Penguin Classics

Skinner, B. F. (1948) *Walden Two* Hackett Publishing Company Indianapolis Indiana

Skinner, B. F. (1984) *News from Nowhere, Behavior Analyst* 8, 5–14 (1985). 10.1007/BF03391908

Smith, Grafton Eliot & Pear Tom (1918) *Shell Shock and Its Lessons* Manchester University Press Manchester

Sophocles (c. 430 b.c.) "Oedipus the King," "Oedipus at Colonus" in *The Three Theban Plays* Penguin Classics (1984) Harmondsworth

Svevo, Italo (1923) *Zeno's Conscience* Penguin Classics 2002 Harmondsworth

Stashower. (1999) *Daniel Teller of Tales The Life of Arthur Conan Doyle* Henry Holt & Company Inc New York

Suchet, David (2013) *Poirot and Me* Headline London

Symons, Julian (1972) *Bloody Murder: From the Detective Story to the Crime Novel* Faber and Faber London

Tallis, Frank (2007) Vienna Blood Arrow London

The Blue Cross, Two Kinds of Paradox, The Queer Feet (1910) in *The Complete Father Brown Stories* Penguin Classics 2012, Harmondsworth

The Detection Club. (1931) *The Floating Admiral* Hodder & Stoughton London

The Ego in Freud's Technique of Psychoanalysis FINISH Society of Psychical Research London

The Secret of Father Brown (1927) and Penguin Classics 2014 Harmondsworth

The Society for Psychical Research "Report of the Census of Hallucinations." *Proceedings of the Society for Psychical Research* 10 (1894): 25.

Tolkien, J. R. R. (1990) *The Hobbit* Harper Collins London

Turnbull, Malcolm J. (1996) *Elusion Aforethought: The Life and Writing of Anthony Berkeley Cox* Popular Press University of Wisconsin Press Wisconsin

Voltaire (1747) *Zadig and L'Ingénu* Penguin Classics 1978 Harmondsworth

Ward, Mary Jane (1947) *The Snake Pit* Cassell & Co London

West, Rebecca (1918) *The Return of the Soldier* The Century Company and Virago Modern Classics 2010 London

Wertheimer, Max (1912) *Experimentelle Studien über das Sehen von Bewegung. Zeitschrift für Psychologie,* 61, 161–265. [Translated as *Experimental studies on seeing motion.* In L. Spillmann (Ed.), (2012). *On motion and figure-ground organization* (pp. 1–91). Cambridge, MA: M.I.T. Press.]

Wertheimer, Max (1922) *Untersuchungen zur Lehre von der Gestalt, I: Prinzipielle Bemerkungen. Psychologische Forschung,* 1, 47–58. [Translated extract reprinted as *The General Theoretical Situation.* In W. D. Ellis (Ed.), (1938). A source book of Gestalt psychology (pp. 12–16). London, U.K.: Routledge & Kegan Paul Ltd.]

Wertheimer, Max (1923) *Untersuchungen zur Lehre von der Gestalt, II.* *Psychologische Forschung*, 4, 301–350. [Translated as *Investigations on Gestalt principles, II.* In L. Spillmann (Ed.), (2012). *On motion and figure-ground organization* (pp. 127–182). Cambridge, MA: M.I.T. Press.]

Wertheimer, Max (1924) *Gestalt theory.* In W. D. Ellis (Ed.), *A Source Book of Gestalt Psychology* (pp. 1–11). London, England: Routledge & Kegan Paul. (Original work published)

Whitman, Walt (1867) *Leaves of Grass*, New York and Standard edition (2017) Race Point Publishing New York

Wilson, Colin & Seaman, Donald (1990) *The Serial Killers: A Study in the Psychology of Violence* Book Club Associates London

Winerman, L. (2004) *Criminal profiling: The reality behind the myth.* Monitor on Psychology, 35 (7), 66.

Index

Printed in the United States
by Baker & Taylor Publisher Services